The discovery

"Somebody made *this, Barney!" crowed Snowy. "Somebody made this just the way they made the steps. There* is *more here! There* is*!"*

"What do you think it is?" I asked.

"I don't know. Looks something like a pathway," said Snowy.

"I think so too." I brushed it cleaner and cleaner. "Leading to the river. And the other way leading back into the cave."

Snowy wiped his sweaty face with his forearm. "Wait," he said. "The steps on the other side of the river? They're directly opposite this road. Maybe nothing's here and it's all on the other side?"

All, I thought. All. What was all *going to be? A village? One little play hut? Was this a joke? Or a model? "Snowy," I said, "you know what?"*

"What?"

"Suppose we're looking at something that no one has seen or touched since before the birth of Christ. Maybe since the Greeks or Noah's ark. How do we ... not wreck it by mistake?"

"An absorbing school story with a twist, this one is sure to fill readers with a sense of wonder." —*SLJ*

SUSPENSE NOVELS BY ROSEMARY WELLS

Leave Well Enough Alone

The Man in the Woods

Through the Hidden Door

When No One Was Looking

through the hidden door

ROSEMARY WELLS

PUFFIN BOOKS

PUFFIN BOOKS
Published by the Penguin Group
Penguin Putnam Books for Young Readers,
345 Hudson Street, New York, New York 10014, U.S.A.
Penguin Books Ltd, 80 Strand, London WC2R ORL, England
Penguin Books Australia Ltd, Ringwood, Victoria, Australia
Penguin Books Canada Ltd, 10 Alcorn Avenue, Toronto, Ontario, Canada M4V 3B2
Penguin Books (N.Z.) Ltd, 182-190 Wairau Road, Auckland 10, New Zealand

Penguin Books Ltd, Registered Offices: Harmondsworth, Middlesex, England

First published in the United States of America by Dial Books for Young Readers,
a division of Penguin Books USA Inc., 1987
Published by Scholastic Inc.,
by arrangement with Dial Books for Young Readers, 1989
Published by Puffin Books,
a division of Penguin Putnam Books for Young Readers, 2002

1 3 5 7 9 10 8 6 4 2

THE LIBRARY OF CONGRESS HAS CATALOGED THE DIAL EDITION AS FOLLOWS:
Wells, Rosemary.
Through the hidden door.
Summary: Two young boys stumble upon the remains
of an ancient underground mystery.
[1. Fantasy.] I. Title.
PZ7.W46843Th 1987 [Fic] 86-24273
ISBN 0-0837-0276-0

Puffin Books ISBN 0-14-230150-7

Printed in the United States of America
Typography by Jane Byers Bierhorst

For Ray Phillips

through the hidden door

CHAPTER ONE

On the day of the earthquake, just a little after three o'clock, Mr. Finney's hated collie, Bonnie, scuttled out of a thornbush yowling in pain.

All six of us stopped and looked on. Since the morning earthquake had been only 3.5 on the Richter scale and hadn't done anything interesting like collapse the school, we had forgotten it by three o'clock. Mr. Finney's collie, going berserk and bleeding from the mouth, or foot, I couldn't see which, was something else.

Her silver paws tore at her teeth and scraped against her eyes. Then she began rubbing her jaw up and down furiously against a slender tree, her tongue skidding in and out of her mouth in agony. I stood with the rest of the boys, dumbly. Afraid to do anything because the collie scared the living daylights out of me.

Rudy Sader, quarterback of our football team, forward on the hockey team, and all-state pitcher, threw the first stone. Rudy was a tall, good-looking boy, with brown wavy hair and strange amber-colored eyes. He laughed at the collie. It was a rich and satisfied laugh. I saw the stone hit the animal in the head. The roots of my hair burst into sweat. Danny Damascus threw the next stone.

This one hit the collie on the side of the mouth. The dog looked up at us for a second, not believing. Then she began to cry and shudder, but she stayed there, still cracking her mouth against the bark of the tree.

We hated that collie, as I mentioned before. She belonged to Mr. Finney, headmaster of Winchester Boy's Academy. We hated Mr. Finney at about the same level as his dog, and we hated his big nosy wife, Dr. Dorothy Finney, who always shot around a corner when you least expected her to, fluttering like some huge kind of poultry. Dr. Dorothy was hard not to bump into. Both Finneys were well liked by most of the boys of Winchester, but my friends and I were not most boys.

The collie had never actually bitten anyone, but the moment you came near her, her lip curled above white teeth, tough as six-penny nails, and she shut her eyes half-mast at you.

"Let's go, guys! Let's go!" I pleaded with my friends. Brett MacRea threw a big fat rock. Matthew Hines and Shawn Swoboda began picking up stones. The next one glanced off the white hair on the very top of the collie's head. Now the dog tried to run away from us, but by this time she had entangled herself, legs and tail, in a grapevine that wound through the thornbush. She lurched, eyes moving wildly, ducking the stones, trying to jerk her body out of the vine, then retching and whining at us piteously, crying for help.

What I did was stand there, in a storm of flying stones and jeering laughter, trying to sound reasonable, almost cheerful, with a trill of panic in my voice. "Come on, guys! We'll get in trouble. Hey! Stop! We're going to get in trouble. Come on, we'll all get Saturday detention!"

Rudy grabbed a dry branch and advanced, doing a little two-step toward the collie. The five boys with me began to yell and laugh and sing curses of all kinds. The dog's big sable-and-white body, usually splendidly brushed, sagged. "Stop it!" I shouted. "You jerks! You're going to kill her!"

The vine had worked upward around the dog's throat. A spray of urine squirted out of her. Her back paws turned lemon yellow where they'd been white.

And all I had the guts to do was stand back with my hands shoved deep in my pockets, shifting from foot to foot, yammering about Saturday detention when the other boys couldn't even hear me for their own noise and the thrashing, strangling animal pinned in front of them.

That was when Snowy Cobb rocketed out of nowhere and threw himself into the bush, losing his thick glasses, which had gone smashing under him. Snowy ripped the vine from around the collie's throat and clucked gentle, soothing noises as he untangled the dog, leg by leg.

Our sudden silence danced in the air with the dust.

"Let's get out of here!" ordered Rudy, and we ran. Oh, did we run. Once I looked over my shoulder. Behind us, rumbling like an elephant through the bushes, clumped Dr. Dorothy Finney, huge-bosomed, and wrapped, as always, in several layers of different tweeds. She matched the late October woods like a camouflaged Jeep. A chain leash jingled in her hand. I didn't know if Dr. Dorothy saw us. I only prayed

Snowy had lost his glasses before he'd had a chance to recognize us.

Alone, I tramped back to the dorm in the cold, covered with the slick sweat of guilt. My friends had gone romping off another way.

I despised my friends. I had since I'd met them. But I'd made no others through the sixth and seventh grades at Winchester. I had skipped lightly and luckily those years. Now my luck had run out, like water skivying down a drain.

When I was eleven years old, I'd been sent to boarding school in the East from Lantry, Colorado, because my mother was long dead and my dad's work took him all over the world.

Lantry is Nowhere, U.S.A. It is sixty-two miles from Denver. We live there because my dad needs the solitude of the mountains for his peace of mind in between business trips. My dad is a westerner by birth, and he needs the West for its open spaces and mountains, but for as long as I can remember, he has told me, "Train your brain in the East, son, just like I did, and then the world will be your oyster." Oysters are squidgy, disgusting things, but this is what he means: Go to Winchester. Graduate with honors. Go on to Hotchkiss. Graduate with honors again. Get into Harvard. Magna cum laude from there and on to Yale or Oxford (as he did), and then you will know so much and meet so many well-connected people that you will be able to go out in the world and make lots of money doing whatever it is you love, which, he adds every time he says this, is the only way to live a life.

I have never argued with Dad's formula because I am too scared of what he says might happen if I veer from The Plan. I might wind up in a nine-to-five job for the rest of my life, taking overcrowded commuter trains, eating a brown-bag lunch at my desk in a cubicle with three other people, and retiring at fifty-five with nothing to show for my life but a gold retirement watch.

So I began my career as an eastern preppy in the sixth grade. With Dad I had traveled to Rangoon, Stockholm, London, and Paris, but never had I been near a rock concert, a sugar maple, or a tollbooth. I didn't know a Nike from a Ked. I was pudgy and freckled, innocent as a kitten. A mountain boy with a nervous lisp, whose only talent was to draw hard-hearted cartoons of my teachers.

On day one at Winchester, Rudy Sader noticed my lisp and nicknamed me Blossom.

The head of the upper form, Mr. Silks, also noticed my lisp. But he hauled me into his office and filled my mouth with selected stones from his fish tank, which he boiled on his office hot plate before every use. With a mouthful of sterile pebbles I recited "The Charge of the Light Brigade," and all of the entries beginning with the letter *S* in the Boston telephone book for forty minutes a day. By Christmas my lisp was better.

In the second semester Silks changed the diet to marbles, also boiled, and started me on Kipling's "If" and all the *S* names in the New York City telephone book. The poem "If" contains forty-nine *S*'s.

In May the lisp vanished, although it surfaced now and then when I got excited. And from May of sixth grade on, no one ever called me Blossom again. Getting a foot into Rudy's gang came by accident.

During the months I'd spent gargling and mumbling my way from Saccarella to Swydoski, Mr. Silks's hair looked quite normal to me. I did not realize that the only place hair actually grew on his billiard-ball head was over his ears, or that he cleverly nurtured the hair over his right ear to a length of about eighteen inches. This long and wide flap he layered and combed smoothly over the dome of his head from the right side to the receiving hairs above the left ear, where they were woven in.

Mr. Silks was also our sixth-grade science teacher. One day I had to do an experiment involving two nickels, an ice cube, a rubber band, and a heat source. I chose a blow dryer for the heat source. During the experiment Silks remarked casually that I was a nitwit. I turned to apologize to him, blow dryer full on. The hair flap wafted right off his head. Then it hung horribly, dangling like a skullcap from over his right ear.

Boys fell on the floor, holding their noses and mouths, keening like widows at a wake. Mr. Silks replaced his hair immediately. He had no choice. In a voice like a police siren he ordered me to copy out the Gettysburg address one hundred times.

Rudy and his friends thought I had done this on purpose. I became a minor hero. Mr. Silks was instantly nicknamed Eggnog, school-wide. After that I leapt at every challenge thrown my way. Rudy's gang accepted me as a comedian and handy brain. From that day in sixth grade on I was a full member. We called ourselves "the guys." The rest of the boys called us "the untouchables." We did terrible things.

Through dinner the night of the dog stoning I sat among my happy, untouchable friends. Sweat covered my body like swimmer's grease. I'd tried showering it away twice. I'd changed my shirt three times, but the guilty dampness spread. The Finneys were nowhere to be seen.

Friday night dinner was always chipped beef on toast. My friends ate as if there were no tomorrow. My stomach shrank to pea size because I was sure there'd be no tomorrow after that afternoon. I began looking around the Great Hall for Snowy Cobb.

I'd never feared anything this much, not even exam proctors, angels of death. I should explain about cheating. In June of my sixth-grade year I found another way of making the gang accept me whole hog. Since then I had prepped Rudy and his friends like a paid tutor for every test and exam, making them lazy and myself indispensable. We did this the night before exams in my room, with me pacing the floor like Hamlet, imitating the teachers' every tic and affliction.

With a rushing heart I'd led these five class leaders through my class notes. I'd shown them how to shorthand all exam information onto Dr. Scholl's Air-Pillo insoles in indelible fine-point marker. During an exam they had only to slip off a Top-Sider to access the whole semester's key jottings like microfilm. This was just one of my seven foolproof cheating systems. Nobody was ever caught.

Danny and Shawn had taken second helpings of chipped beef, which we called chipped barf. Weren't they even thinking about their future? I prayed that the collie was alive and promised God then and there I'd never help them cheat again. If the collie was dead, I wouldn't have a snowball's chance in hell of getting into Hotchkiss, my dad's alma mater, the following year for high school. Once you go to one "right school," and Winchester is one of the rightest of schools, getting into the next "right school" is as spine tingling as applying to college.

Rudy Sader would lose his scholarship to Winchester and never make Lawrenceville. He'd wind up back in his hometown high school. This would be death for Rudy's dream football career. The mothers in Rudy's hometown were an aggressive bunch who'd bumped football out of his high school's sports program on the grounds it was dangerous and bred mental illness. There would be no Choate in Danny Damascus's future. No Taft for Hines or St. Andrew's and Groton for Shawn and Brett. Cheating at Winchester carried a penalty of instant suspension, or expulsion. Was trying to kill the headmaster's dog on a level with cheating? I guessed it was worse.

I tried to bury my alarm by shoveling large forkfuls of lukewarm beef into my dehydrated mouth. It stayed right there, curdling. I choked, just like that poor damn collie.

"Oh, God, save me," I whispered for the seven-hundredth time. *Why should God save you?* answered the voice of my conscience. *You didn't lift a finger to save that suffering dog.*

High over my perspiring scalp was a ceilingful of names. Inscribed on the vaulted apse of the great hall, in silver script, were all the brave, dead Winchester boys who, unlike me, had grown to manhood and then died in the service of their country. The list went back to the War Between the States. I supposed that if I were ever drafted into the Army, I'd end up court-martialed for cowardice under fire. The toast I'd packed into my mouth churned like cement in a dishwasher. Were the Finneys having a private funeral in their backyard? I excused myself and ran to the boys' room.

I was sick as a dog, head over the toilet bowl. The word *dog* again. Was she fighting for life in some vet's operating room? The Finneys had no children of their own. They doted on Bonnie. And where in hell was Snowy Cobb?

Evenings, senior boys on honors are free to roam anywhere on campus until lights out. I was a senior boy on honors. My last night of it, I was positive.

Snowy Cobb was a sixth grader, two years behind us. I figured he'd be in required study hall. I glided past the study hall door like a ghost and looked in through the small wired pane. No Snowy. No Snowy in the library either. *Of course he isn't there, you geek,* I told myself. *He broke his glasses. The lenses are half an inch thick. They'll probably have to send out to a special ophthalmologist in Miami or Toronto or wherever he lives to get another pair. The poor kid will miss a week of work and then have to study double to catch up.*

I headed into another bathroom and threw up into another toilet. *God, why can't You turn me into somebody else forever?* I asked. *I'll take a body with a handicap. Be a street beggar in Turkey. Somebody from a Communist country.*

In the hallway I ran into Rudy. "Hey, Barney!" he said, whacking my backside. "What's goin' on?"

"I'm looking for Snowy, Rudy," I said.

"Yeah? Why?"

"Rudy, we could be out of here by tomorrow night. Suspended! Expelled! Don't you realize that? We've got to find out what happened to that dog."

The next thing I knew, Rudy's massive tanned arm hugged me close around the shoulders.

"Hey, cut it out!" I said. "I'm serious."

"Yeah? Well, *you* cut it out, fool!" he said. "You even open your face in front of Snowy about the dog and he'll know for damn sure who was there. You want us all to hang, you bimbo?"

"Okay, okay, Rudy!" I sputtered.

"Got it, Blothum?" Rudy teased me, not yet letting go of my collar.

"Cut out the nicknames, Rudy. And let go of me. I'm thinking of our future, for crying out loud. You want to go to a football-free high school?"

Rudy unhanded me with a warning smile. "Nobody's gonna know," he said. "Nobody's gonna find out. Snowy can't see his own dick without his glasses. We were all down at football practice at three this afternoon. Okay?"

"But how are we going to prove that, Rudy? There's other boys. They'll say we weren't there. How about the coach? Mr. Redfearn won't lie, he—"

"Look, Barney," Rudy said like a rug salesman, "no sweat. Redfearn's in my pocket, okay? Something happens to me and the boys? There goes his season and the conference championship. Redfearn needs me, man. No sweat."

"I hope you're right, Rudy."

"Believe me, Blothum!" whispered Rudy in my ear.

Danny Damascus slipped into my room at about midnight. Naturally I hadn't been able to sleep. I lay in a cocoon of moist sheets, a piece of fluff up my nose. My tongue felt like a wool mitten, and I was beginning a sty on my upper left lid.

"Hey, man!" said Danny cheerfully.

"I can't thleep, Danny!" The words bubbled out of me. "I have to know what happened to the dog."

"Barney, the dog's okay. God's truth. Just a few scratches. I checked it out."

"How'd you check it out?"

"Went out the kitchen entrance. Biked downtown. Looked in Finney's front window. Dog's curled up in front of the fireplace. Sleeping like a baby," said Danny. "Not even a Band-Aid on him."

"Her!" I corrected him. "Danny, are you telling me the truth?"

"Truth! Saw it with my own eyes. So sleep, kid. Okay? And kill that goddamn speech defect before Silks yanks you in for a round of his gravel therapy!"

I thought of how much I had shared with these boys, of how close I'd been to them and all their rottenness.

I twisted around in my twisted covers. "But even so, Danny. If they find out who did it—"

"No one's gonna listen to poor blind Snowy," said Danny. "And the rest of the boys—they know better than to rat on us. They might get hurt. I'm a nose tackle, baby. I can hurt a lot of people, and no one's gonna be quick enough to see. Accident. Easy. The boys know."

Easy was how Danny drifted out of my room. I slipped to the floor in my sheet cocoon and fell asleep there.

I dreamed, oddly, of an earthquake that measured twenty on the Richter scale, in the middle of Greenfield, Massachusetts.

Not only did the whole school crumble upon itself, ivied walls and stained glass windows shattering, but it went down in a shower of flying Right Guard deodorant, video cassettes, Frequent Flyer coupons, and PC jr.'s. Top-Siders spun through the air, forever parted from their mates. J. Press blazers blazed. Navy blue rep ties with the school crest knotted themselves around the branches of our two-hundred-year-old elms, and the molten sinuses of the earth filled like candy dishes with Binaca breath spray, graphite squash racquets, and Yale sweat shirts with the sleeves carefully ripped off at the shoulder.

I woke at five, halfway under my bed. Senior boys on honors are allowed private rooms. I had one.

Tomorrow, if I were still at Winchester, I'd be rooming with a lower former or maybe three of them.

I dressed in track sweats and crept downstairs. Then I trotted across the common and three miles into Greenfield, down Hancock Street to the Finneys' house. Only an orange cat, flicking his tail from a fence top, took notice of me.

Four times I circled the house, each time trying to peer in without seeming to. Finally I hid in some juniper shrubs under the living room window, popped up, and looked in for one and a half seconds.

No collie slept by the fireplace. Nor in the familiar chintz-covered wing chairs. I'd had formal Sunday tea in that living room a dozen times with Finney and Dr. Dorothy. The collie usually growled at us boys from behind a gateleg Hitchcock table. But the collie wasn't there either. I sprinted out of the bush and back toward campus. Since I detested jogging and only did it when the coaches forced me to, I knew I'd live on aspirin for a week.

"I'll jog all year if it'll make you happy, God," I gasped, my breath steaming, tears welling in my eyes. "Please, God, let that dog live. I'll do anything if you let that son-of-a-bitch collie live unharmed. If you help me, God, I'll give my year's allowance to the ASPCA. I'll save the whales when I grown up. If there's a next life, I'll volunteer for a hitch as a Tibetan yak herder. Somebody has to do it and it will be me (pant), Barney Pennimen (huff), and I'll give my yaks (puff) expensive food! I swear to God, God."

CHAPTER TWO)

Inlaid mahogany bookshelves lined Mr. Finney's office, floor to ceiling. Scattered among the calfskin-bound volumes were Indian pots and a couple of model clipper ships. The rug was a purplish Sarouk, worth a mint, and the chairs dark squeaky leather, ancient, British, grand. In one of them sat Mr. Finney, full bellied, white eyebrowed, and smoking a pipe that had gone out. In the other, Mr. Silks, hair in place, diddled with the finial on a silver humidor.

"Sit down, Pennimen," said Finney, pointing to an uncomfortable straight-backed chair, from which he promptly removed both his feet. The feet dropped with a thud. One leg was said to be wooden.

I tried to shut off the trembling in my hands by exchanging glances with an Indian mask with a horsehair moustache. If the mask was real, I priced it at about five hundred bucks.

"Talked to your father, Pennimen," said Finney, emptying a dollop of black gook out of his pipe and stuffing it with long shreds of tobacco. "He hopes we can straighten this out." Finney's gentle blue eyes lit on mine like lasers. What awful things had he told my dad?

"So now," Finney said, "exactly what happened yesterday afternoon, Pennimen? Think hard. One lie and you will not only be scratched from Hotchkiss next year, you'll be out of Winchester tomorrow. Back to where the deer and the antelope play."

I began to cry.

"Stop that!" shouted Silks. "Immediately!"

"Leave him alone, Martin," said Finney, striking a kitchen match on the sole of his shoe. "Cry away, Pennimen. It's emetic."

"What's emetic?" I managed to sob out.

"If you were to swallow a cigar butt," he explained, "I would give you syrup of swills. Then you would be good and sick. The cigar butt would be thrown from your system, and you'd feel much, much better. Syrup of swills is an emetic. So is crying. Now. Tell me what happened without shilly-shallying around. Who threw the first stone at my dog?"

"I did. I was the only one who did," I answered as grittily as I could, tears beginning to run down my cheeks and snot dripping from my nose.

"Come on, Pennimen. I'll only kick you out for a good lie." He pulled heartily on his pipe and blew out four perfect smoke rings. They would have been bull's-eyes around my nose if we'd been playing horseshoes. "We've spoken to Clarence Cobb, Pennimen. His vision isn't particularly good, and his glasses busted before he could see who the boys were, but he did tell us one thing. There were five or six boys. One of them was trying to stop the others apparently."

Clarence, I thought distractedly. So that's what his real name was. "How could he tell if he had no glasses?" I asked in a sudden tenor voice. "Snowy's as blind as a bat."

"So he is. He is legally blind without his glasses, as a matter of fact. But his hearing's awfully good. He told us one boy was jumping up and down yelling at the others, 'Thtop! Thtop or we'll get Thaturday detention!' This boy was not throwing any stones at all. He had some good intentions. This boy could only be you, Pennimen. Who were the other boys?"

"I don't know who they were," I droned like a microwaved Nathan Hale.

"Pennimen, what did I say about lies?"

I wondered if he and Silks could smell me. "One lie and I'm out of here, sir."

"That's right. This is your last chance. Give me your right hand."

"My hand?"

"Your hand. Put it right flat on mine. That's it. Now look at me. That's right. Now we'll start off slowly. Okay?"

My God, I thought. *The man's a human lie detector.* But my eyes didn't dare waver from his.

"Your name is Barney Pennimen?"

"Yes."

"How old are you?"

"Thirteen and one month, sir."

"Who are your friends here?"

My hand discharged a pint of sweat into his. "Rudy, I guess. Danny Damascus. Matt, Shawn, Brett MacRea."

"Good. Keep your hand there on the table." Finney wiped his palm on his pants and slapped it back under mine. "Is it true, Pennimen, that two years ago you poured a quart of vodka into your housemaster Mr. Greeves's vaporizer while he was asleep?"

I breathed very deeply and shut my eyes. "Yes, Mr. Finney."

"I thought so. Was that your idea?"

I wondered if the statute of limitations had run

out. My hand felt like a freshly caught mackerel. "No," I answered.

"I see. Was it true, Pennimen, that a year ago you stole the March of Dimes donation card off the counter at the Liggett drugstore and spent the money in the video game machines at the movie theater?"

"Yes, Mr. Finney, but I returned it by mail with five dollars extra put in."

"Was stealing it your idea? Open your eyes and look at me, Pennimen."

"No," I answered.

"Is it true, Pennimen, that you have been seen pulling all kinds of wild mushrooms out of the ground and eating them willy-nilly because Rudy and his friends dared you to?"

Visions of past emergency-room nightmares ran by me. "Yes."

"Has anyone ever told you that you could kill yourself eating wild fungus?"

"Yes, Mr. Finney."

"Then why did you do it?"

I began to cry again. "I don't know."

"Have you ever cheated in an exam, boy?"

"No. Yes. Well. I've never cheated myself, but I let other boys make cheat sheets from my notes."

"Why did you do that?"

"So they'd like me." I began to gag. I stopped it by driving my fingernails into my palms. *You're a human banana,* I told myself.

"By doing that, even if you don't cheat yourself, you are robbing honest boys of top grades. Do you know that?"

"I . . . I didn't think of it that way."

"Answer this question."

"Yes?" I swiped at my streaming eyes and nose with my left sleeve.

"Did you throw any stones at my dog?"

"No, sir."

"Who did?"

Sobs from me.

Finney peppered his next words one by one, like darts. "Do you think it was cruel, beastly, disgusting, Pennimen, to torture a helpless animal like that?"

I could not speak. I nodded vigorously.

"Name them, Pennimen!"

The strangling collie appeared in my mind's eye. My stomach turned and I threw up again, right on the priceless Sarouk. Finney didn't seem to notice. Silks's body began to twitch like a rabbit's nose. "Sader," I said softly, gulping. "Damascus. Hines, Swoboda, MacRea."

"Who threw the first stone?"

"Rudy."

"Clean up your mess or I'll fry your ears, Pennimen," said Silks.

"Mr. Silks, it'll take an hour and alcohol-based cleaning fluids. This rug is worth thirty thousand bucks," I said.

"What are you talking about, you cheating, lying little devil?" Silks asked, standing. When Mr. Silks got angry, his face reddened from the bottom up, like a jar being filled with cherry juice.

"Easy, Martin. The boy's right about the rug. His father's an antiques dealer. Mail order world wide. Pennimen even does the drawings for his father's catalogue. Get some newspaper from that table," said Finney gently, emptying his pipe into an ashtray and then spilling the ashtray on the floor. "Put it over the mess. We'll clean it up later." He looked at me.

"Mr. Finney, how's the dog?" I asked.

Finney sat back in his chair and looked at me quizzically, tapping his pipe stem on his front teeth. "Good for you, Pennimen," he answered at last. "The dog is fine, or will be. You just saved your neck, by the way."

"How?"

"By asking 'How's the dog?' rather than 'What will my punishment be?' An unfeeling boy would have looked after himself first."

I didn't react to this slight ray of sunshine. Finney went on. "The dog had jammed a bone between two of her teeth and couldn't get it out. As for the stoning, she has some cuts that will heal. Her trachea, that's the windpipe, was badly bruised. She'll have a plastic tube in it for three days, until she can swallow and breathe properly again. She'll be home Thursday. As for her future attitude toward boys, I can't say. This brings me to what happens to you."

"Yes?" I swallowed hard, wishing the plastic tube were in me instead.

Silks picked up the telephone and ordered somebody at the other end of the line to round up Rudy and the rest. I only prayed that I would be long out of the headmaster's office by the time they showed up.

Over Silks's voice Finney went on. "You acted stupidly and shamefully, Pennimen, but you were not craven or savage like the other boys. You certainly weren't brave like Clarence Cobb."

"I know, Mr. Finney. I am sorry from the bottom of my heart . . . I can't say anything else."

Finney passed a tobacco-smelling handkerchief

across to me. "I'm glad you are sorry. I hope you mean it. I hope you're sorry for all the other things you've done too."

"I promise never—"

"We'll see. You have been extremely stupid. You're lucky to be alive after eating a bunch of toadstools. Despite your good grades you so far have a record at Winchester of being a total idiot as far as I'm concerned. And dishonest. But I have never wrecked a boy's life when he tells the truth. So . . . Saturday detention for you until Christmas. All honors canceled. All privileges and free weekends canceled until semester's end. Up in the morning at five thirty for kitchen duty for the next six weeks. None of it on your permanent record if you have a clean sheet from now on. I will not destroy your future at Hotchkiss just because you've been a blockheaded ass."

Silks had been wiggling to say something. He slammed down the phone. I didn't allow him to catch my eyes with his. I stared instead at the leather tassels on his loafers. "All right, Pennimen," he began, "I want you to learn something about suffering."

"Yes, Mr. Silks."

"You go to the library. I don't want to see you outside that library for the next month."

"Yes, Mr. Silks."

"I want you to write me a hundred pages on the ten worst disasters in history. I want the black plague, the wipeout of Mexico City. I want tidal waves, famines, floods, and avalanches. Got it? Now get out of here and start writing."

There was a slow, grudging knock on the office door.

"That'll be Rudy Sader and friends," said Silks.

I thought I would dissolve, like a germ in a dish of penicillin.

"Go out this way, Pennimen," said Finney, and grinning, he pushed open a window to the outside.

CHAPTER THREE)

Sader and Damascus were in my room when I got back from the library at ten. Finney had expelled all five untouchables from Winchester.

"I didn't open my mouth, guys! Finney's old lady saw us. Dr. Dorothy saw us," I told them over and over. When that didn't work, I lied more colorfully. "Silks put my fingers in a finger vise and got it out of me."

"Yeah?" said Danny. "Let's see your hands."

Oh, why hadn't I prepared myself? Lying effectively means good groundwork, like preparing for an exam. I could have roughed up my knuckles a little. Dragged them through the driveway.

"Not a mark on his hands!" said Danny. "The turd is lying. How about I show you what I can do to your hands, huh, creep? I'll break each finger for you four ways."

Rudy put out a restraining hand. "We can't touch him now." He smiled broadly at me. "Not yet," he added. "But we want you to know fear, Blossom. We want you to stink of fear. Got that? Because some day, some way, I'm gonna get you, and then Danny's gonna get you, and after that your own mom won't recognize you."

"My mom's dead," I said.

"Yeah? Well, how would you like to pay her a visit?" said Danny sweetly.

During the next three days I might have been on the dark side of the moon. No one in my class talked to me and I talked to practically no one. The five boys had left the campus. I spent almost all my time in the library, taking notes on the bubonic plague of 1348. At night, I was exhausted from morning kitchen duty, which got me up long before sunrise.

Then suddenly, Saturday morning at breakfast, mimeographed slips were on everyone's plate. They explained that Mr. Finney had resigned because of a sudden illness. Mr. Silks was to take his place as headmaster and had taken the oath of office that very morning, so to speak. By noon Rudy and Danny and the three others were back. They played first string against North Hampton Prep that afternoon, with Rudy at quarterback.

At four o'clock, when I left the library, I noticed orange-topped stakes in the ground in one of the empty meadows near the school. I went over to have a look. On the seat of the pickup truck that was parked along the road was a clipboard. The top paper on it was an invoice reading, Karlo V. Damascus Memorial Swimming Pool, Winchester Acad.

That night the school was heaving with rumors. None of them was true but one. Rudy, Danny, Shawn, Brett, and Matt had been granted full pardons for whatever it was they had done. Not many people seemed to know exactly what that was.

Next morning I went right to Mr. Silks. The headmaster's office had been transformed overnight. Gone were the rug and the leather chairs and the Indian art. No calfskin-bound volumes lined the walls. The bookshelves themselves had been taken down. The office was painted avocado and harvest gold. The furniture was grisly Danish modern.

"I know why you're here, Pennimen," said Silks. "Your punishment stands."

"But the others!" I pleaded. "They got off scot-free."

"That was a decision of the board of trustees," said Silks. "You were given a punishment by the former headmaster. I see no reason to lift it."

I knew that arguing would probably get me a bath in the septic tank. Still I said, "But, Mr. Silks, it isn't fair."

"You'll find one thing changed here, Pennimen," said Silks.

"Yes, Mr. Silks?"

"We don't like whiners, tattletales, toadies, or stool pigeons here at Winchester."

"Yes, Mr. Silks."

"You put liquor in your housemaster's vaporizer, Pennimen. Possession of liquor is grounds for expulsion here at Winchester, not to mention all the other tricks you've pulled."

"But they did them too. All of us did those things. This whole mess started because of the collie, and I didn't do anything to the collie."

"I believe that, Pennimen, like I believe the moon is made of green cheese. You were in it as much as they were. All you did was wiggle off the hook and point the finger at the other boys. I make it a policy never to believe a boy who rats on his friends. If I'd been headmaster last Monday, I'd have thrown you out of this school so fast you wouldn't have seen the door slam in your face. If you don't like your punishment, go to the board of trustees."

I shifted my feet and stared at the floor. I didn't

know the board of trustees from the Chicago White Sox.

"While you're in the library, Pennimen, look up Kipling's poem 'If.' The one we read first term to cure your speech defect. Memorize it by Monday. Every morning before class I want you to come in this office and recite it to me. You hear me?"

"Yes, Mr. Silks."

"If I can train a boy not to lisp, I can train him out of other bad habits. Now get out of here. You make me sick."

The next week and the week after I closeted myself in the Herbert J. Vanderbilt Library when I wasn't in class, on kitchen duty, or washing walls. No one in school talked to me by then. Rudy and the gang spread it far and wide that I had squealed on them. The whole school now called me traitor.

Vanderbilt Library was the pride of the school. It had more Corinthian columns, books, and microfilm, I reckoned, than the whole state of Colorado. I wondered if, at some distant time in the past, Herbert J. Vanderbilt's son or grandson had been kicked out of Winchester and miraculously brought back in by means of this wonderful library.

Different boys came and went, researching papers and looking things up, but one boy was always there. It was Snowy Cobb, elflike, his skin bronze and his hair white blond. School rumor said that his mother was a famous Greek opera singer and his father a Norwegian fisherman. Or maybe his father was a Greek fisherman and his mother a Swedish opera singer. The name Cobb was a mystery. At any rate, he sat off in a corner. He consulted only a set of ancient blue reference books and used a magnifier to see what was on the pages. He took no notes. On his desk, at all times, he kept a small grayish object.

By the third Saturday in November I was up to my third disaster, India, a famine that killed three million. No one but Snowy and I were in the library that afternoon. The whole school had gone thirty miles away to cheer the team on as they faced Our Lady of Perpetual Help Middle School in Amherst. I prayed that Our Lady herself was watching the game and would personally see to it that Rudy got sacked painfully ten times and that Danny ran into a goalpost.

During the hours I'd spent in the stacks Snowy had not once raised his eyes to me or said a single word. Frequently I'd found myself staring at him, unblinking, as if I were gazing at a fire in a hearth. I decided that either Snowy was afraid of me, or he plain hated me.

But what was he looking up so feverishly? What was the little gray thing that he kept putting down on the pages? I would never have found out and everything that followed would never have happened except for a slow-flying hornet that started buzzing over Snowy's head. He swatted at it, and his magnifier fell and smashed on the floor.

Snowy bit his lip. Then he knelt and began picking up the bits of glass. He swore softly. I cleared my throat. "Bad luck," I said. "When's your paper due?"

He glanced at me coldly from under his soft cornsilk hair. I figured he couldn't weigh more than sixty pounds. After a little he decided to answer. "It isn't a paper," he grumbled.

"What is it, then?" I got up from my desk and ambled over to him.

"Research," he snapped.

"On what?" I worked my way over to his desk.

"None of your business." The little gray object on his desk was a bone. Tiny and all scratched up. It was no bigger than a joint on one of his fingers. The reference book was opened to a skeleton of a rhesus monkey. The text was in Latin.

"You read Latin?" I asked. He couldn't have had much more than two months of Latin IA.

"Go away," said Snowy. "Go away and be with your friends."

"Snowy, they're not my friends anymore. They've threatened to kill me because I ratted on them. That's why I spend my afternoons in the library instead of checking books out. I'm scared to be anywhere on campus alone."

Snowy closed the book with a slam. He began tracing the foil-stamped design on its cover with an index finger. The big hand on the library clock clucked the passing minutes several times before he opened his mouth. Finally he muttered, "You have a reputation of being thoroughly rotten. Mr. Silks said in assembly that certain boys were thoroughly rotten, and everybody knows who he means."

"I am thoroughly rotten," I said miserably. "But I'm trying to be better. My life isn't over yet. At least I hope it's not."

Snowy opened the book again and flattened the spine. "That's not the page you were on before," I said. "This is a lemur. You were on rhesus monkey."

"This is the rhesus monkey."

"No, it isn't. Can't you see . . . " I stopped myself. Of course he couldn't see. His magnifier was gone.

"Would you like some help?" I asked. "I can read this pretty well."

He shifted in his chair. "I guess so," he answered.

"What are you looking for?"

"See this bone?" He held it up. "It's a leg bone from something."

"Where'd you find it?"

"It was in Mr. Finney's collie's mouth. I went with Dr. Dorothy to the vet when we got the dog untangled. The vet pried it out from between two of the dog's teeth. It took him a good fifteen minutes to get it out. When the bone fell out, it dropped on the floor. I picked it up and put it in my pocket."

"And now you're trying to find out what it's from?"

"Well, yes. You see, it looked strange to me. The next day I showed it to Mrs. Glickman, in science class. She told me to go to the library and find out what it was. I haven't found it yet, but at least I'm safe here from Sader and Damascus. They're after me too, you know. I keep looking. This is my two-hundredth skeleton. The bone doesn't match with anything."

"How do you know it's a leg bone?"

"It's just a guess. It looks just like the femur, the upper leg bone in the human skeleton."

I shrugged. "Then it's got to be a monkey of some kind."

"Yes, but all the monkey leg bones are curved and thin." He pointed to one of the drawings in the book. "This is a straight bone, and thick."

Again I shrugged. "How old do you think it is?"

"I don't know."

I picked the bone up off his desk. From what I'd seen of museums of natural history and a few science books, it did look like a leg bone. It had scratches and grooves up the shaft to the knob, which was cracked and half gone. "Can't be very old. There were never great apes or missing links a zillion years ago in Massachusetts, I don't think. It *must* be from a monkey." I ransacked my feeble store of knowledge. "But this wasn't ever, you know, a jungle or anything. I'm sure no monkeys ever lived here. It must have come from somewhere else. But how could a monkey get here? In the middle of Greenfield, Massachusetts?"

"Could have been a pet," said Snowy. "Mr. Finney says it might have been brought by a sailor who got it in Africa in the old days. It might have been an organ-grinder's monkey."

"Mr. Finney! Where is Mr. Finney?"

"In town. I visit them nearly every night after supper."

"But I thought . . . They said he was sick!"

"He's not sick. He resigned in a big huff. There was a meeting with the school trustees after he expelled Rudy and Danny and the gang. At the end of the meeting Mr. Finney ripped off his necktie, the one with the school crest, and threw it on the floor in front of all the trustees and stamped out of the room. I heard the whole thing."

"How? Where?" I asked.

"You know the boys' lavatory in the old building, next to the common room?"

"Yes."

"The north wall of the boys' room backs up on the wall of the common room. First they made me come and talk to the trustees. Bunch of old men in pinstripe suits. They asked me questions for a while. About what I saw when the dog was attacked. Then they told me to leave. I went out and stood on a john in the boys' room and listened to the whole rest of the meeting right through the wall with a water glass over my ear."

"Well . . . go on."

"When I was in the meeting, before I listened through the wall, I told the trustees what happened, same as I told Mr. Finney before. I told them five boys I could not see well enough to recognize were torturing the dog to death. I told them a sixth boy with a lisp was trying to stop the others. That's all. Silks said that there were no boys here at Winchester who lisped. The men decided it was five words against one. Mine. They also said throwing a few stones at a dog was a boyish prank and not worth two cents compared to selling dope or something serious. Finney protested that he ran the school. He was headmaster and the boys had been expelled and that was that. The trustees said Finney was going to wreck Winchester's chances of winning a conference championship in football, hockey, and baseball if Rudy and his friends weren't on the teams. They also said that Mr. Damascus had just made the kind offer of an indoor swimming pool for Winchester. They've been trying to raise money for the pool for a long time. That's when Finney stamped out of the meeting.

"When it was over, I went back in the common room. I found Finney's tie on the floor. I know it was his because his Navy tie clip was still on it."

I didn't see Snowy for a week after that, although I waited for him every afternoon and evening in the library. My interest in tidal waves and volcanoes had flagged to the point of no work at all. Instead I began going through the fat volumes of Snowy's Latin encyclopedia of natural history. Nowhere in any part of any skeleton did I find a bone even close to Snowy's.

I next saw Snowy just before an English class. I asked him where he'd been. "Mr. Finney took the bone," he said, "and sent it off to a friend of his at the University of Massachusetts. They have something called a carbon dating department there."

"What's that?" I asked.

He scrunched his nose under the bridge of his glasses. "It's a way of finding out how old something that was once alive is. U. Mass. sent it back. They did the test as a special favor for Mr. Finney. According to the guy at U. Mass. they get a thousand and one bones sent in from all over the world every month. People find things in their backyards that they think are prehistoric saber-toothed-tiger skulls and they turn out to be groundhog's jaws."

"Well, go on," I said impatiently, but I was beginning to learn that Snowy could not be rushed.

"It's old, all right," said Snowy. "Maybe even a hundred thousand years. They don't really know. Their test goes back only fifty thousand years. The test could have been wrecked by the dog's blood and saliva that soaked into the bone."

"A hundred thousand years! Wow! What kind of bone is it?"

"Well, that's the thing of it. The guy said it looked like a primate. Since there were no monkeys or anything ever found here in Massachusetts, it must have come from somewhere else. Been dropped, like Mr. Finney said."

"But an organ-grinder's monkey doesn't have hundred-thousand-year-old leg bones," I argued.

"Doesn't matter," said Snowy. "Somewhere out in California they found eighty-thousand-year-old bone knives and arrowheads. The bones are Stone Age all right, but they were only carved up by Indians many, many centuries later. The Indians just found some ancient bones lying around and whittled them. The guy at U. Mass. looked at the marks on my bone and said it had pretty likely been carved. Maybe a hundred years ago by Massachusetts Indians here, copying a human skeleton. Mr. Finney says probably some early Indian tribe used to carve human skeletons as part of a religious burial ceremony. Or maybe a sailor traded for it in China in 1850. Massachusetts had a lot of ships coming in from all over the world. Or maybe South Yemenis carved it after a monkey skeleton and a traveler brought it to Greenfield five years ago. Maybe someone else did.

"Anyway, all the stuff they've dug up in Africa looking for the missing link and all that junk? Well, it was discovered pretty recently, but it was there in the earth forever. This could have been buried in Australia or Lapland or Japan, then carved to look like a leg bone and brought here."

"So we'll never know," I said sadly.

Snowy didn't answer this. He held the bone up between his thumb and index finger. "It could have been carved," he said. "But then, it got some rough sawing inside the collie's mouth, and that could have made the scratches."

"U. Mass. doesn't sound very interested," I grumbled.

Snowy dropped the bone in his shirt pocket. "Since they figured it was brought here from somewhere else and the dog could have picked it up anywhere, they said there was no sense in going around looking for the whole skeleton. Mr. Finney talked to them on the phone. They don't have the money to study every single bone. I'm late for class," he added, and dashed away down the hall.

For the next week and a half, until it was nearly Thanksgiving, Snowy disappeared again, but wherever he was, I guessed it had something to do with the bone. The funny little bone had me by the short hairs too, and I knew if I were to have any time at all to spend on it, I had better finish up my disaster paper. I did. I made it one hundred and nineteen pages. I don't think Silks bothered to read it. He did not return it to me, nor did he do anything but grunt and look daggers at me when I showed up mornings to recite "If."

The night before Thanksgiving break I lay in bed, my mind full of skeletons, labeled in Latin, all drawn before the First World War, of wild boars and antelopes, gorillas and Shetland ponies.

An idea circled my head like a fly. It had to do with Snowy's bone, but it was fuzzy and I could not get hold of it. Was it only this, that because of a tiny unknowable little object my mind had begun to work beyond cheating rings, friends I hated? I let myself think of my father, when he and I had discovered an early Cézanne crammed in a dusty bassinet at the back of a San Luis Obispo thrift shop. Dad and I had celebrated that night, as if we'd been Balboa and son and had just discovered the Pacific Ocean. I meandered down the corridor to the john. Yes. That was just how I felt about the bone.

We had to find out where the dog had dug the bone up. There my thoughts stopped.

I threw myself back in bed, wondering how I could explain the bone to my dad.

In my bed was a body. Before I could scream, big hands slid around my throat and over my mouth, cutting off my voice. Then, wildly laughing, Rudy leapt from the bed and left the room. "Didn't want you to forget about me!" he whispered with an awful giggle.

CHAPTER FOUR)

By Thanksgiving morning my father had settled his rage enough to talk sensibly to me.

Silks had written him every detail of my miserable record, from mushroom eating to cheating rings.

Dad picked me up at the Denver airport. In the car he said I deserved to be belted within an inch of my life, but he didn't believe in hitting. Maybe he should have whacked me when I was young. I might have turned out better. He called me a jackass, a fool, a moron. He asked me to explain each of the dumb things I had done.

"Because I wanted them to like me, Dad," was all I could answer to every question.

"But why? Why *them?* Why choose the lowest scum of the earth to be your friends?"

"Because they teased me when I first came. They made fun of my lisp. I knew it would go on like that for three years unless . . . unless I somehow joined up with them."

From that point Dad went on about being an absent father. What would have happened if my mother had lived. He called himself worse names than he did me.

At three thirty in the morning we decided to take a walk.

"Sky's so big out here," I said. "You forget what it's like when you're in the East."

"Can you put this behind you, Barney?" Dad asked.

"Yeah."

"I don't like you going back to a place with a half-nutty prison warden like Silks in charge. I don't like five linebackers twice your size prowling around till they wring your neck. I don't like you being punished and not them, and it makes me puke to hear about Papa Damascus and his stinking swimming pool."

"Can't do much about it, can we?" I said. "I mean, I can't switch to another school midterm with my record. I can't live home with Uncle Edward and go to Red Arrow High."

"Pit Bull High," said my father.

"What?"

"They've changed the name. The football team's now called the Red River Pit Bulls. They're putting up a twelve-foot-high statue of a bullterrier between the cannons at the entrance. They wanted it on the roof, but that got voted down."

We watched the sun come up behind the mountains.

"There's a school in Monterey, California," said Dad after a while. "I know the dean of students. He collects old glass. I could get you in there."

"I'll stay, Dad. I'll stay where I am and keep my nose clean and somehow go to Hotchkiss."

"You can be three thousand miles away from Silks and Sader and Damascus."

"I'll think it over, Dad," I said.

We walked until dawn warmed our backs.

I covered miles that weekend, through the still streets of Lantry in jeans and an old poncho. I took a horse out and rode in the mountains. I had been far from Colorado for a long time and wasn't completely at home there anymore.

Boarding school is where your center is, and once you're part of it, you can only get halfway home again. Home is still where your family is. Home is still where your bedroom is. But that bedroom is changed once you leave. I've seen it in my house and in other boys' houses when I've spent weekends. Things in our rooms are thrown away the minute we leave home. There are no month-old septic Pepsi cans lying on the desk. Piles of mildewed underwear vanish like spring snow. What our parents think are disgusting and violent posters are removed from the wall. Beds are freshly made and tucked in, and a permanent month-of-March smell pervades everything, just the way it does in a guest room. Home becomes school and school becomes home.

As I sunk my teeth into a leftover drumstick Saturday night I knew I would go back to Winchester.

Dad sat cross-legged on the floor in front of the fire. He lit a cheroot. "You won't consider Monterey?" he asked.

I shook my head and gnawed on the turkey leg. "Monterey's for rich basket cases who couldn't pull a D average at Winchester," I said. "I looked it up in the town library in Peterson's *Secondary School Guide.*"

"So does Peterson's tell you flat out it's for rich basket cases?"

"No, but it lists the SSAT scores for Winchester boys. Average is high six hundreds. Monterey's average is low three hundreds. Monterey goes through grade twelve. They got only one kid out of two-hundred-and-fifty graduates into an Ivy League school last year. It's the pits, Dad. They don't offer Latin, and they give credits for surfing and bird watching. It's all there in black and white, Dad. In Monterey you major in braiding lanyards."

"God, Barney, what a snob you've become!"

I shrugged, selected a turkey wing, and muttered, "Once you get on the roller coaster, you stay for the whole ride, I guess."

"It's my stupid fault, Barney," my dad said. "I've brought you up to think you have to go to Winchester, Hotchkiss, Harvard. Just because I did. You don't have to do anything you don't want. Maybe you'll want to be a beach bum someday. Or a carpenter. Or even work, God forbid, nine to five for IBM."

"I want to go back East."

"Only because I've drummed it into your head for thirteen years."

I finished the turkey wing. I found myself looking at it critically. It made me think of the little leg bone back in Massachusetts, sitting in Snowy's locker. "Yup," I answered him. "But it's too late now, Dad.

I'm a twenty-four-carat Yankee prep. Ice water in my veins and I sleep in button-down Oxford-cloth pajamas from L. L. Bean."

"Those boys might try to break your kneecaps, Barney. I'm serious. I'm afraid they may kill you. These things happen."

"I like Winchester," I said.

"Then you're as nutty as a fruitcake." Dad stood. "C'mon," he said, and led the way to his huge studio at the back of the house, where he kept and catalogued his finds.

He showed me a pair of elephant tusks that had once framed the doorway of a raja's palace in India. There was a gold pocket watch inscribed to King Edward VII from Queen Alexandra on their wedding day in 1863. On his latest trip Dad had picked up a number of Malaga cabinets, over three hundred years old, from Spain, which he was just unpacking and inspecting. But the best he saved for last.

"What is it?" I asked.

"It's what they used to call a lady's pistol," he told me. He put it in my hand. The butt was no bigger than my palm, and the barrel did not reach beyond my index finger. "Sterling silver veneer," Dad added. "Found it in a collection of Victorian hats, of all things. It was sitting in the bottom of a hatbox. Got it for three pounds. Worth about eight hundred."

The silver had been tooled with flourishes and the design of a peacock on either side of the handle. The peacock's eye looked to be a tiny jewel.

"That an emerald?" I asked.

"Yup. But only on one side. The left side, where you can get at it with your finger easily. The other eye is green glass. Took me a while to figure it out. Then I realized that if you touch the emerald eye, it cocks the trigger mechanism. Guns like this were meant for a lady's hand and a lady's purse. But in case the gun was grabbed away, the assailant couldn't use it against the lady unless he knew the trick mechanism."

"You mean it works?"

"Better believe it works. Try it."

"Is it loaded?"

"With little tiny slugs," said Dad.

I aimed it at a carton full of Styrofoam packing chips in the corner of the room. *Kapow!* went the gun. *Kapow!* five more times. The bullets went right through the carton and deep into the wood of the wall beyond. "What are you gonna do with it, Dad?"

My father took the gun back. He loaded the

chambers with six more slugs. Then he dropped it into a red, white, and blue U.S. Olympic team joggers' pouch, the kind with a zipper and a Velcro belt that runners wear to keep their loose change in. "I'm going to give it to you, Barney," he said.

CHAPTER FIVE)

Sunday night after Thanksgiving I searched all over the dorm for Snowy. Boys trudged by me, trailing puddles of slush water from their boots, crowing happy insults, and walloping their luggage against the walls of the dormitory. I snaked past them.

I waited in Snowy's room until his roommate came shuffling in with two duffel bags slung over his shoulders. "You looking for Snowy?" asked the skinny sixth grader.

"Where is he?" I said.

"I don't know."

"Well, did he go home for Thanksgiving?"

"Snowy doesn't go home much." The sixth grader sighed. He was pale-faced with a shock of straight black hair that fell over his forehead. I'd seen him. I did not know his name. He dropped the duffels on the bed, unzipped them, and gazed mournfully at the hopeless jumble of clothes inside. "His mom and his dad are divorced or separated or something like that. His mom's in France, I think, or one of those countries. His father's in Canada or Mexico, I forget. Maybe California or Italy." He sniffed. "Snowy never tells you much. You know? He's living off campus now. Switched to being a day student. Trying to get anything out of Snowy's like trying to . . ." His thought dribbled away.

I waited, sitting on the bed and pulling shirt after shirt out of one of his duffels for him. "Well," he went on, "trying to get to know Snowy is the same as trying to get ice cubes out of one of those rubber ice trays that don't work."

I nodded, pulling out more shirts. The shirts had been crisply ironed. The trouble was they'd been packed in a giant ball.

"Still, it's good for me, isn't it? I mean, I get a single room now, just like a senior boy."

I asked him if he knew where Snowy was living off campus.

"Nah. He never says. I'll be glad to get rid of that skull collection, though."

"What?"

The roommate pointed to an empty shelf. "He used to keep skulls on that. Squirrel skulls, raccoons, stuff he found in the woods. Even a snake skull and backbone. He was weird. I mean, I know his IQ was a hundred and eighty or something, but he gave me the creeps. Look at the stuff he reads!"

Here Snowy's roommate handed me a pile of magazines. "You keep them," he said. "I'm tired of seeing them around. It'll be nice to have some room here for my stuff." He cleaned a swath through the grime on his dresser top with the sleeve of a fresh shirt, sneezed at the dust he raised, and wiped his nose on the same sleeve.

I lugged the magazines back to my room. I let them drop in a heap at the back of my closet but at the last minute pulled off the top one. Kneeling there, I leafed through it. Weak, spindly, half-blind Snowy, I could see him poring over the anatomy books in the library. If he'd had a subscription to *National Geographic* or *Ranger Rick,* I wouldn't have thought twice. But these had nothing to do with the Snowy I knew. These were something I'd never known existed.

They were back issues, forty or fifty of them, of *Soldier of Fortune.*

Soldier of Fortune was crammed full of stories about little wars that I had no idea were going on, all over the world. They certainly never came up in current events class. The men who fought these wars were not sent by the U.S. or any other Western government, they were on their own. Doing it for money and the fun of battling Commies.

These were stories on killing leftover Vietnamese, patrolling the borders of Nicaragua, driving off Cuban battalions in tiny African countries the names of which I couldn't start to place on a map, and hand-to-hand combat in the Libyan desert. Was this real? It seemed to be. I read three stories. In them one man was squeezed to death by an Amazon River boa constrictor, two others fell over a waterfall in Tanzania, and five more were blown up in a land mine set by Manchurian insurgents. Just what the Manchurians themselves were insurging about was not clear.

Snowy had gone over the texts with a yellow highlighter pen and marked everything of interest with exclamation points. Gentle, quiet Snowy. The magazines were loaded with ads for everything from Uzi hand-held machine guns to blow darts. You could buy a half-wolf German shepherd puppy or a complete medicine-growing farm to prepare for the day when all the pharmacies closed down. In among the back pages were printed order forms that he had ripped out. What had he ordered? Tarantula repellent? A bulletproof vest? A tiny microphone that let you listen to conversations a quarter mile away? Yes, yes, I decided suddenly. Something had rung untrue in Snowy's story about listening to the trustees' meeting where Mr. Finney had stomped out. The boys' lavatory did not back up against the common room. There was a broom closet in between. The only way he could have overheard the meeting was in the bushes outside with a seventy-five-dollar listening microphone in the palm of his hand.

The *Soldier of Fortune*s had not been mailed to Snowy at school. The address printed on the backs was care of the local post office, general delivery, in the name of Mr. Robert Cobb. I pushed them deep into my closet and piled a bunch of last year's math workbooks on top of them. I had stumbled on to a secret of Snowy's. I intended to keep it to myself.

During the night I woke once, recalling several photographs in the pages of the magazines. They were of groups of men, standing or sitting with weapons in hand, all blurry. All black and white. I couldn't see their faces well, or even tell what kinds of uniforms they wore. From time to time Snowy had circled one or another with a ballpoint pen, adding a little question mark each time.

I didn't find Snowy until Tuesday afternoon, when he'd passed me a note in my mailbox saying to meet him in the old school stables at two thirty after classes.

There hasn't been a horse on campus, the gym teacher once told me, since the Second World War. The rose brick stable at the edge of the woods has been a storehouse for the school grounds keepers in the meantime. It is covered with creeper vines, untrimmed, and I could see at least ten birds' nests hanging empty in the fall sun. Inside, there are twenty lonely stalls. Still, the horseless air smelled of rotting hay, and in one stall a yellow-toothed rat peered out at me from among the cobwebs.

"Snowy!" I called. No Snowy.

I began poking around. Opening cupboards. Finding bits of moldy riding gear not quite interesting enough to touch. *Am I afraid?* I wondered for a second. *No. I have my pistol.* That morning I had strapped it tight around my upper right thigh and torn out the right-hand pants pocket so I could reach it. I did not like wearing a gun. "A complete easterner is what you've become!" my western dad would have said.

It was true. Dad had taught me to shoot when I was eight. Guns were as common as pencils in the West, and I had grown up with them, but the eastern view of guns had seeped into me. I thought of them now as the toys of macho slow-brains and redneck wimps.

I unstrapped the pistol in its red, white, and blue pouch and buried it in a deep mass of black humus that had gathered on a windowsill in the first of the empty stalls.

"I thought you wouldn't come," said Snowy, suddenly coming up behind me after I'd looked in every stall and called out his name five times.

"Where were you hiding, Snowy?" I had a feeling he'd been there all along, watching me.

"I wasn't hiding."

"Then what's happening? And where are you living off campus?" Snowy was maddeningly secretive.

"I found out where the bone came from," he said.

"Where? How?"

"Over Thanksgiving I spent the four days with the Finneys."

"Snowy, are you living with Mr. Finney and his wife?"

Snowy gazed out the doorway and kicked some straw, both his hands deep in his front pockets. "I took the collie out. I took her for runs day and night. One afternoon she led me to where she found the bone."

"Where, Snowy? Where?"

"I won't tell."

"Come on, Snowy. You dragged me into this. That's not fair!"

"I'll take you there. But I'll only take you because I need help."

"Help?"

"I will need help soon, anyway. I need an intelligent aide who can keep his mouth shut. I picked you because you're smart and you want a place to hide away from Sader and Damascus and their friends," Snowy said. *Intelligent aide,* I thought. Snowy's vocabulary comes right out of hand-to-hand combat in the Libyan desert.

"You're right there," I answered. "I can't stay in the library after school forever. Sader and the guys are staring right past me these days, but I know they're just waiting for a chance to get me alone. I guess I'm smart enough—I have a three-point-nine average. And I won't say a word to anyone."

Snowy went on as if I'd said nothing and he was recruiting the head of a brigade. "You must swear on your honor as a man and an American never to tell a living soul what we find, never to remove anything, and I'll only lead you there blindfolded."

"Blindfolded!"

Snowy opened his hand. In it was a black disk the size of an Oreo. "I carry a listening device to make sure we aren't followed," he said. "Take it or leave it, Barney."

I took it. He wound the back of an old black soccer shirt over my eyes, tied it in back, and secured it above and below with masking tape. Then he walked me around the woods for three quarters of an hour, never more than five minutes in any direction and with several complete three-hundred-sixty-degree turns. "This is ridiculous!" I yelled at him several times.

"You want to come or not, Barney?" Snowy answered each time. Finally he got me on my hands and knees, gave me a string end that led to his belt, and then told me to fall on my belly and crawl through an opening. "You can take the blindfold off now," he said after a minute's crawling. "Don't lose it. Put it in your pocket."

I ripped off part of my eyebrows with the tape.

We were in a kind of basic darkness. Blinded, I thought I would suffocate too. "Where in hell are we?" I screamed. "Get me out of here!"

"Don't be afraid," said Snowy. His feet shuffled on just ahead of my face. "We're in a cave. Or we will be soon. Follow me."

"A cave! I hate caves! Do you have a flashlight?"

"Of course. A little one. And Sunday afternoon I brought down a kerosene lamp. I left it here."

I struggled along through the clammy mud tunnel after him. Panicky not to get stuck in the darkness, I yelled, "Turn the stupid flashlight *on,* Snowy!"

"Not yet."

"Tell me why not!"

"Because this is only the entrance, Barney. There are other ways to go after this tunnel. I don't want anyone to know which way it is. If you take the other ways, you can get lost in here forever. I found the cave and I want it to stay secret. Don't worry. I know just where we are. I can hear where we are by the sound of the water."

"God save me." I choked on my words and a clayey mouthful of soil. I heard water too, but what it meant or where it was gushing and dripping from I couldn't begin to imagine. The tug of the string in my hand told me Snowy was moving. "Let's go," he said.

"Turn the *light* on, for God's sake!" I begged him.

"Wait. Follow me."

Snowy turned me twice around and then led me down a walkway. It turned out to be a ledge. I felt outward with my left foot. There was no ground, only air beneath it. "Snowy!" I pleaded, clinging with my fingernails to the wall beside me and balancing on my right foot. "In the name of God will you put the bleeping light on!"

"I was just going to," said Snowy. He flashed it on the ceiling of the tunnel.

Above us twinkled a thousand iron-colored icicles of rock, dripping water like faulty shower heads. Twenty yards or so beneath my dangling left leg identical red-brown icicles grew pointing up.

I had come within a hair of tumbling sixty feet down, smack onto a grove of sparkling limestone bayonets. When this registered in my brain, I peed straight down my leg.

Think of springtime, Barney, I told myself. The ledge we crept along was as narrow as my shoulders. I needled myself with singsong advice. *Which are the stalactites and which are the mites? Don't look down—you'll fall off. Don't shake—you'll fall off. And remember to breathe or you might as well fall off right this minute.*

Drip drop, drip drop went the ceiling. The slithery rock wall beside us was as comforting as a dead man's arm. Suddenly the path ahead ended in a hole.

"Slide!" Snowy shouted. I did, with my stomach just behind my teeth. I counted the seconds that my backside bumped down the chute. Seventy-five seconds. "Snowy! Snowy!" I cried. "How will we ever get out of here? We can't climb back up this. It's too steep and slippery!"

"Another way!" echoed Snowy's voice.

We bumped to a stop on a patch of soft sand. It felt like a beach at the North Pole.

"Stay there," Snowy said. He untied the string from around his waist and let it fall. Then his flashlight dipped and weaved farther and farther away from me as he moved deeper into the cave.

I sat in the sand, my pants frigid and wet. "Don't leave me, Snowy," I wailed. "I'm sorry I didn't rescue the dog like you did. I know I'm just a gutless wimp! I'm a rotten louse and I know it. But don't leave me!"

Snowy didn't answer, but soon there was a glow of light from a spot not so far away. It flared and illuminated the space all around.

We were in a vast sandy-bottomed cave, covered by a roof domed as perfectly as a planetarium's. Down from the ceiling hung fat, drunken columns of tiered stone. They glistened in the lamplight and looked just like upside-down stacks of glass pancakes.

The floor of the cave, as far as I could see in all directions, was powdery mint-colored sand. I played with a handful of it but couldn't tell if the greenish kerosene light altered the color. Somewhere beyond the reach of the lamp a river ran. Snowy loped toward me, swinging his lamp and marveling at the huge secrecy of the place just as I did.

When he came up beside me, he asked, "Still scared? Well, don't be. We're perfectly safe. I'll take you home soon."

"But how come . . . " I began. "There aren't supposed to be any caves around Greenfield. We'd have a science trip to them if there were. We'd at least have heard about them. There's tourist brochures on everything else around town. How—"

"The dog led me. I just followed her."

"But why hasn't anybody else—"

"Mr. Finney says it was the earthquake back in October. Right at the entrance to this cave is a rock that must have moved slightly. I can tell because there was a tangled-up bunch of dried moss over the slit where we crawled in. Just as if it had been pulled away. I've carefully stuffed the crack with new earth and moss. No one could find this place again, Barney. Even I couldn't find it if I hadn't marked it when the dog went in the entrance under the rock. All the wild places, rocks and hills and stuff, look alike out here. So I marked it secretly."

"Then why blindfold me?"

"Because if we keep coming back here again and again, you might know where the entrance is after a while."

"But so what? And why should I want to come back here again and again?"

"Barney, something's down here."

"What?" I shouted at him.

"You'll see. But first, look around at the sand."

"Okay. Sand is sand."

"Right. You see my footprints. Where I'm taking you you'll see my footprints and the dog's from a couple of days ago. That's all."

"So what?"

"The rest of the sand is as smooth as a beach after a full tide's gone out. See! The sand in here has a little crust. Nobody has been in this cave at all. If they had been, they'd have left footprints. You can't go onto a beach and then walk back and leave no footprints. When I followed the dog here, Barney, there were only her footprints in the sand. Not a grain had been disturbed other than the dog's paw prints."

I shifted uncomfortably in my damp pants and looked into the darkness that lay around us. What had Snowy found? Why was he dickering around with me like this? I wanted to say "Get to the point!" but I didn't. Instead I picked up a little crust of the sand where it lay untouched and broke it between my fingers like bread.

"How do we get out of here?" I asked him, my fears welling up suddenly again.

"Don't worry. It's easy. We walk out, practically, through another tunnel. The exit is in another part of the cave. But we'll always come in by the slide down, Barney, because if you ever find out how we get here, if the blindfold slips, if anybody ever follows us, you'll know how to get in, but not out."

"How did you find the way out? You could have been trapped in this place forever!"

Snowy smiled but didn't answer me. He turned around, and I followed him over to the bank of the river. The water ran as black as India ink. "There are fish in there," he told me. "If you shine the light just so, you can see them swim." We followed alongside for several hundred yards. The cave did not end. Was it miles big? Finally Snowy pointed to a spot in the sand where he'd left a garden trowel. "Look," he said.

"I don't see anything."

"Wake up, Barney. I'm the one who's supposed to be blind. Look there."

I got down on my hands and knees. "Is this where the dog led you?" I asked. I couldn't think of anything else to say because what I saw made no sense at all.

Snowy nodded. "I've dug all around here with the trowel. There's nothing else but that. Maybe somewhere else there's more. What do you think of it?"

Leading from where I was kneeling down to the edge of the water was a set of twelve marble stairs, each no bigger than half an inch high and two inches wide.

"This is impossible, Snowy," I said.

"I know," Snowy agreed. "But it is . . . well, it *is* there and all."

"It must have been an Indian toy, a game, maybe an Indian ritual of some kind. . . . Just like Mr. Finney and the guy at U. Mass. said. Maybe it's what kept the squaws busy when the braves were away hunting. Maybe they made sort of architectural models of things before they built them full-scale."

"Maybe," said Snowy. "Except Mr. Finney told me about the Indians who lived here before the white man came. They were Mohicans. They built wigwams. Nothing like this."

"Another tribe. Before the Mohicans."

"How about the bone, Barney?"

"Well, this explains the bone just the way the guy at U. Mass. said. The Indians made it by carving up a much larger piece of bone," I reasoned, logical explanations darting around in my head like gnats. "You ever see how the Chinese can carve up a piece of ivory? With tiny castles and pagodas and dragons? The old ones are worth a fortune. You could carve any bone you wanted with your eyes closed if you took the time. It was probably part of some death ceremony."

"Barney," said Snowy, "feel the steps. Close your eyes and feel the surface of them."

I did as he told me. "What of it?" I asked. "They're stone. What am I supposed to feel?"

"Barney, the middles of the steps are worn."

Needles of electricity frisked through my fingers. My heart was still and light, and I knew I would come back and back and back, though the cave would be like Antarctica in winter and I'd probably go through the tortures of the damned living up to Snowy's strange rules. I would come back until I knew what else lay here deep under the sand and how a set of tiny steps had come to be built in a place that might not have heard a human voice since time began.

Snowy doused the light. In complete blackness he

led me by the hand, then turned me and turned me until I had no sense of direction left. We walked over some sand, but then I felt rough stone underfoot. *No footprints,* I thought. *He's making sure I don't know the way out.* For five or six minutes we made our way on the uneven rock, until we slipped into a passageway at the edge of the cave. We followed a labyrinth that led on like a slimy-walled funhouse, Snowy gliding through the dark, me stumbling behind him. The tunnel seemed to lead around the perimeter of the cave, but I wasn't sure. He blindfolded me at the last place we could stand up. Then we crawled out the way we'd come in.

Outside I could not see any better through the blindfold than I could in the cave's darkest places, but I felt the weak sun on my face, and I grabbed hold of a piece of tree branch, just to make sure it was there.

"So what do you want to do, Barney?" asked Snowy.

I sucked in the deepest breath I could, let it out, and said, "Holy Christmas, Snowy. We've got to find more!"

CHAPTER SIX)

Exploring the cave was not going to be easy for me. Looming ahead was not a delicious winter of exploring but a dangerous one of after-school sports. Sader and Damascus controlled the hockey rink, Hines and Swoboda the basketball court, and Brett MacRea ruled wrestling. After my disaster paper was done, Silks had stopped me in the hall and said I'd better show up for winter sports if I didn't want to become a lazy slob in addition to everything else I was.

Through the school grapevine everyone knew Snowy Cobb wasn't expected to take sports because he couldn't see a beach ball coming at him from ten feet away. I was healthy, but I knew my former friends well.

Someone had stolen Rudy's cleats one year. Rudy waited till after football season was over. Two well-aimed pucks and a couple of bone-numbing checks with a hockey stick brought the cleats back and put the thief in a rubber neck brace for three weeks. Someone else had once got on Brett MacRea about his zitty complexion. Brett spiked him so badly on a slide into second base in a practice game the following day that the boy wound up with twenty stitches and played late-inning right field for the rest of the season. I didn't want to imagine what Brett could do in a wrestling match. I took my chances with basketball. I also took my dad's advice on being dealt a bad hand of cards. Bluff for a while, then fold and wait for the next deal.

Our first practice game was the day after Snowy showed me the cave. I bluffed, feinting, leaping, pretending to go for it like a rookie on the make for first string. Twenty minutes into the game Swoboda slammed me in the solar plexus with an elbow while I was in the middle of a jump shot. The coach's back was turned. At first I couldn't tell whether Shawn meant it, because he reached down to give me a hand to my feet, good-buddy style. Then his eyes lit up with a jewel-like gleam that said, *This is a warning, squealer!* I did not get to my feet.

By the time they got me to the infirmary, I was quite well again. As a matter of fact, when I'd gotten back my wind, I was fine. But why say so? *Every cloud has a silver lining,* I told myself, so I lay in my cot and moaned, remembering the details of what Dr. Feinstein says when my father throws his back out. All twelve Budweiser Clydesdales couldn't have dragged me back on the basketball court.

The doctor came at eight. By then I'd had time to go over the whole nine yards of bad backs—sciatica, weak links in muscle chains, hateful rehabilitative exercises in the morning—as if I were preparing for a science test.

I complained of a knifelike throbbing in my lower back on the right side. I pointed where the shooting pains radiated down the sciatic nerve on the back of my right leg. I winced because my groin was involved and the entire pelvic cavity felt hot inside.

Naturally the doctor lifted each of my legs in an arc. At exactly forty-five degrees measured on any pocket protractor I screamed so loud the doctor jumped.

"You have a back spasm, young man. Do you know what that is?" the doctor asked.

"No! It hurts."

"Of course it hurts." He listened to my chest and took my blood pressure. "The human back is like a chain," he said, a hand on my shoulder. "One weak link and the whole thing goes. You're lucky you didn't compress a disk."

I rolled my eyes at him.

"I'm afraid you'll have to give up sports for a while."

"That's not fair!" I said.

He left me with some pills and a booklet of exercise regimens.

Silks came by after that. I think he gave me a little test. "Anyone push you down, Pennimen?"

"Not on purpose, Mr. Silks."

"Good. Good. No sign of that lisp creeping back, eh?"

"Oh, no!" I answered. "Thanks to you."

"Good. Well, see you back on the basketball court soon, I hope."

I prayed Mr. Silks would not have a cure for back spasms the way he had a cure for speech defects. "As soon as the doctor lets me," I said as encouragingly as I could.

"Good. Meantime you're still due to lose your private room. I've dug up a roommate for you. Sixth grader. Name's Mellor. Used to room with Cobb."

"What happened to Snowy Cobb?" I asked

smoothly, wishing he'd found a larger and neater person for me to room with.

"Cobb's a day student now. Moved into town. Night, Pennimen."

Next morning at eight Peter Mellor spread his possessions all over my room. He owned a replica of every team's football helmet in the NFL. Twenty-eight helmets complete with bulky face guards. Try as he might, he couldn't fit them all on the shelves together, so he chose to display one conference at a time. This still gave me no shelf space, but Peter, unlike my senior classmates, at least talked to me and was a live body in the room in case Rudy or one of the boys had ideas about getting me at night. Peter even showed sympathy for my back, or maybe it drove him nuts that I was forced to miss sports. He told me gravity boots had cured a linebacker of the Miami Dolphins of a fused spine. He'd read it in *Sports Illustrated.* Gravity boots would get me back in basketball right away. I told him I didn't think there were any gravity boots on campus. No problem, Peter answered. Krazy Glue a pair of ski boots to the doorway. Do a headstand on a chair. He would get my feet locked in, and I could hang for fifteen minutes. My back would fall into place. I said I had to do a five-hundred-page paper on South American agriculture. I told Peter it would take me all winter in the library. I was preparing him for my absences in the cave.

When I got Snowy's note in my mailbox next morning, I was idiotically happy. At two thirty I limped conspicuously all the way to the caretaker's shed and picked up two large flashlights and a heavy trowel, as the note specified. From there I made it unseen to the stables in half a minute at a sprint.

I didn't argue with the blindfold. I took it as solemnly as medicine. I didn't argue during our roundabout trip through the woods. I didn't scream in the tunnel or wobble on the ledge. Snowy and I did not talk until we were in the cave and at the site of the twelve small steps.

Then, as in the days to come, I felt that the cave was half mine, anyway, even if I didn't know its location. When we were working, Snowy and I were brothers. In the outside he was suspicious of everything.

Whatever else was in the cave, besides the steps, was hidden under a sea of sand. We dug at random, with garden trowels, all around where the steps were, as deeply as the soft green sand allowed. There was nothing. Snowy tried another place twenty feet away. I did the same in another direction. Again not so much as a pebble appeared in our trowels.

All in all we dug over fifty holes in the sand without a crumb to show for it.

"There's got to be something here," said Snowy. "There just has to be more than those steps."

I sat back on my haunches. "Next time we need a kerosene stove," I said. "It's so cold down here, my fingers are stiff."

"I can buy one," said Snowy. "I have money."

"Okay. And five gallons of kerosene."

"But what good will it do if we can't find anything?" Snowy asked.

"I think we're not going at it the right way. I think just digging holes here, there, and everywhere is probably dumb."

"Well, what is the right way?" Snowy asked. "I mean, the whole place is sand. It goes on for miles, like a desert. There's nothing to see on top of the sand. I'm not a dummy, Barney. I looked up in the library how lots of old cities and things were found."

"How?" I asked.

"Different ways. Mostly there were big mounds on the landscape, you know? Sticking up. Some guys a hundred years ago just kind of went up with a bunch of camels and natives and chipped away and found all this fabulous stuff. Sometimes they just dug under cities that were already there. Like Jerusalem. Sometimes they had old maps and books by the Greeks that gave 'em an idea of where to look. Anyway, as far as I could tell, there was always a hump or mound or some clue to lead to the right place. All there is in this cave is just level sand. Acres of it. We could spend ten years."

"How did you find the steps?"

"I just walked along the riverbank. I didn't see them, I stepped on them. I looked down after I felt something hard under my foot."

I spat. I took up handfuls of sand and let it filter through my fingers. Thinking.

Snowy went on. "I mean, we could dig forever and not find anything if we go on like this."

One more time I tried to make sense of the little steps. "Supposing," I said to Snowy, "the steps had a reason for being right by the river. What do you think steps next to a river could be used for?"

"Used for?" said Snowy. "I thought you said they were miniatures made by the Indians."

"That's what I mean. Why did the Indians put them there?"

"You mean, why were they put here, even as part of a model, sort of?"

"Yes. Why would they lead down to the water like this?"

"A dock, maybe."

"That's all I can think of. But a dock would have been carried downstream or disintegrated long ago."

"So," I said, "a cajillion years ago this might have been a toy dock. And now there's nothing left. Nothing anywhere. Maybe everything but these stairs was made of wood and has gone *pfffp!* Snowy, why do you think there's any more than this? This has got to be some kid's game. So a kid carved up a set of stone steps. So what? Could have been done five years ago, for all we know. Maybe a kid found the cave and never told anyone."

"Barney, I told you there were no footprints when I first came down here. You could see for yourself there were only my prints and the dog's."

"Maybe," I said. "But the ceiling drips here, and it's damp air. In five years, ten, maybe our footprints would settle in the sand and a crust would form from the moisture. That could happen in six months."

"Until this October there was no cave entrance, Barney. That rock that moved in the earthquake is the only entrance to the cave."

"How do you know? There may be other rock overhangs, other crevices . . . "

"I checked the inside of the cave, Barney. It took me four days. The way we come in is the only entrance. The way we go out connects to it. There's a small hole in the ceiling about half a mile away, but no one could come in that way because it's about a hundred-yard drop to the floor and the hole's only as big as your fist. It's the way the bats go out."

"Bats!" I said, my skin popping out in a cold sweat.

"They won't hurt you. They're on the ceiling. The first day I was here, the dog barked for some reason, I heard them on the ceiling and I shone my light on them. Then I watched them fly out at about five thirty. They all go through that tiny hole like bees going into a hive."

"Bats carry rabies!" I said, standing up and looking at the ceiling nervously.

"C'mon, Barney. Don't be such a paranoid. They're harmless. As long as we don't frighten them with loud noises."

I still felt uneasy about them. I began pacing in a circle.

"Are you about to give up?" he asked. "Because

you're scared to death of a few bats like some geek who won't walk under a ladder?"

I stamped, rubbed my chapped hands, and stuck them under my armpits for warmth. "It's hopeless," I said, dodging his question. "How are we going to find anything in this . . . this freezing underground desert? Even in a parka and a vest I'm cold."

"It's not hopeless," Snowy said. "We just have to keep at it. Boy, I'd hate to be with you in a lifeboat."

"Why?" I asked.

"A little cold and a few perfectly nice bats make you a quitter," said Snowy. "We've got a chance to make the find of the century here, Barney. Something nobody's ever seen before. And you're going to quit."

"Snowy, at best it's just some toy thing made by Indians. If there was anything else, we'd have found it long ago."

"It's not a toy thing, and it wasn't made by Indians."

"How do you know? What do you think it is?"

"If I told you, you'd laugh."

"I promise not to."

Snowy too was stamping and rubbing his hands. "Forty years ago, Barney," he said between his teeth, "some guys, some U.S. Marines, landed on an unoccupied island in the Pacific. Okay? The island wasn't even on a map. Only one guy survived. The island was inhabited by a race of pygmies."

"Come on, Snowy."

"This is the truth!"

"Okay, okay."

"The people were no bigger than up to your knee."

"Okay, what happened to them? How come *National Geographic* didn't go out there and take pictures, huh? How come they haven't been on TV?"

"Because the Japanese bombed the place to pieces, that's why. The one American guy who survived and told about it had a piece of shrapnel in his head this big. No one believed him."

"So how come you believe that story? Where did you hear about this?"

Snowy wouldn't tell me. I knew it was straight out of the pages of *Soldier of Fortune*, and *Soldier of Fortune* was worse than the *National Enquirer* to me.

I was about to say, "Forget it. Take me home," but I thought flickeringly of Rudy and the boys. Some afternoons there were no sports practices. Special assembly days we got out at three thirty and had free time to ourselves. Weekends with no away games the untouchables were around campus. They were biding their time. If I wasn't in the cave, they'd find me. They'd find me sure as hell. Besides, just supposing Snowy found something and I wasn't there to see it. "You felt the steps," I said slowly. "Supposing we walk around in our socks. Maybe we'll step on something else."

"Let's be organized this time, Barney," said Snowy, his voice happy again. "We walk in squares, okay? Maybe ten yards on a side. Then we walk in rows up and down, filling in the square. The way you mow a lawn. That way we miss nothing."

We padded over the sand in oblong patterns, marking the crust with our sock prints and coming back every few minutes or so to warm our feet by the kerosene lantern. "Why don't we build a fire? It'll be as warm as a stove," I said. "The cave's high enough so the smoke won't bother us."

"Are you kidding?" asked Snowy, shambling along in a careful line. "That's all we'd need to drive the bats crazy."

"Just how many bats are there?" I asked, trying to sound neutral and unafraid.

"Hundreds," said Snowy. "Mr. Finney says bats

often spend the day in caves. They have very sharply hooked claws so they can hang on to the stone ceiling."

"Bats!" I repeated. "I don't like bats! I don't like sharply hooked claws either."

"Well, don't look up. They're asleep. Have you found anything with your feet yet?"

"No. Just sand. Freezing sand."

CHAPTER SEVEN)

Snowy and I paced off our squares for three days in a row, starting at a corner and walking in smaller and smaller squares at each go-round. It was every bit as much fun as vacuuming an Astroturf football field. Each time we came up empty. Then, on Sunday afternoon, I suggested to him that we go across to the other side of the river. As neither of us had rubber boots, we rolled up our pants and ran barefoot through the water, which was so cold it seared like boiling fat.

We paced out the same squares on the other side. The river water had been so unbearable that even the freezing sand felt warm. We hadn't brought our stove across and so could only walk for about five or six minutes before we thought our feet would solidify and frostbite would set in.

"No good doing this anyway," said Snowy. "My

feet are like blocks of ice. I wouldn't feel it if I were walking on broken glass."

I agreed. I took off my socks and tried to rub some blood back into my toes. Then my hands got so cold I had to hold them under my armpits again to warm them up. The socks were frozen from putting them on my wet feet after we'd run through the river. I didn't have the heart to put stiff, icy socks back on. I jammed them angrily in my parka pockets.

"Let's go," said Snowy, and he made a mad dash, splashing through the river to the stove burning invitingly on the other side.

I followed him. "We're doing something wrong," I said sadly. "I don't know what it is, but we're not going at this the right way."

Snowy mulled this over. Neither of us had an answer. "Next time we wear duck hunter's boots," he muttered. I pounded and rubbed and kneaded my poor feet and only managed to anesthetize my hands again. When I jammed my hands in my pockets, wiggling my fingers for circulation, my legs froze next to the pockets.

The next day, in Army issue jungle boots supplied mysteriously by Snowy, we hauled the stove across the river and marked out areas that must have amounted to nearly an acre with orange-topped surveyor's stakes. Snowy had stolen two dozen from the site of the Karlo V. Damascus Memorial Pool. Snowy had also brought two pairs of hunter's socks that he'd no doubt also ordered from *Soldier of Fortune.* They were wired to heat up like electric blankets. The socks were wonderfully warm, but neither Snowy nor I stepped on so much as a single pip in another three acres of the frigid, softly crusted sand—that day or on any other day that week.

Miserably I tramped back to the stables, blindfolded and led by Snowy, on Friday afternoon.

"What are you thinking, Barney?" Snowy asked.

My brain was as cold and useless as my frozen fingers. All it told me was *Dead end. Give it up. Dead end. Give it up,* as flatly as my little cousin's Speak & Spell. "The hell with it," I snapped. "We're never going to find anything, Snowy. We're beating a dead horse. Who knows what the bone is or what the steps are. We'd have to be scientists to find out."

"Don't quit, Barney."

"Snowy, what good is it? We're just a couple of schoolkids. We don't know anything."

"Barney, please!" Snowy's voice was like a little boy's. A far cry from the one in which he usually gave me orders like a sergeant.

I promised myself I'd call Dad that night. I was

tired of hiding out from Rudy and Company in a bone-frosting cave. I was tired of Snowy and the digging. If Dad could get me into another school after Christmas vacation, it would suit me just fine. A semester of surfing in Monterey looked very good that afternoon. No Rudy or Danny. No Silks. No freezing, frustrating caves. Dad was right. Muddy water had dripped onto my head on the way out of the cave. My hair stood up in ice spikes. I looked like a unicorn—a multicorn. California would be a very good place to go to school, I decided. *Chicken!* said a voice in my head.

Mellor, who went skiing every weekend with his Boston family, had dumped in the hall enough filthy laundry to clothe five boys for a month. I took off my clay-streaked shirt and dirty socks and threw them in the pile. My pants had seen five straight cave trips. They were in terrible shape due to the slide and the mud tunnel. I turned out the pockets, because the laundry won't do your pants unless the pockets are free of spitballs, chewing gum, and dead lizards. I threw the pants in the pile and remembered the dirty frozen socks, in the pockets of my parka, from earlier in the week. I tossed them in too and strolled down the hall to wash up.

My hands were filthy, with slight bleeding around the base of every fingernail due to tunnel crawling. I ran them under the warm water. Just before I reached for the soap, I noticed little pellets or nodules of something on my nails. I took the pellets off and automatically saved them on a wad of Kleenex, telling myself to toss them out.

I began whistling "California, Here I Come." Then I opened the Kleenex and stared at the four reddish peas. I couldn't figure out where they'd come from since no hard bits had shown up in the sand in the past five days. Our feet were warm and sensitive in the hunter's socks. We'd even examined the bottoms of our feet with the flashlights after every turn around the squares.

Since it was Friday afternoon, most boys were gone for the weekend. Those who hadn't left for home had all piled into a bus and gone to a Christmas dance at a girl's boarding school forty miles away. Off limits for boys on probation like me. There was not much for me to do. Unwillingly I wandered down to the science room, all the while mumbling to the air, "Give it up, Barney. It's just a couple of pebbles." *The first pebbles we've found,* said the voice in my head.

So what? I answered.

It won't hurt to try and find out what they are, will it? wheedled the voice.

Fine. But I'm not going back in that Siberian cave.

Give me a break! the voice said.

I reached Snowy by phone at eight o'clock.

Snowy met me at the stables first thing the next morning. On a sun-filled window ledge I spread out two wads of tissue and a magnifier I'd borrowed from the science room cabinet.

Snowy squinted through his awful glasses into the magnifier. "What are they?"

"What do they look like?" I asked.

"I don't know. Tiny pieces of reddish-brown something. The top edge shiny and with some bluish . . . paint?"

"Right. Now look at this." I put another chip next to the others.

"Same thing. Paint, or whatever it is, is black, though."

I pocketed both. "You know that fake Greek vase in the main hall, Snowy?"

"Yes, I know the one. How do you know it's fake?"

"Are you kidding? A forty-gallon amphora, black figures on red, in perfect condition? The thing would be in the Metropolitan Museum of Art if it were real. They keep it full of dried cattails and straw flowers. Even Silks isn't that dumb. If it were an antique, the school could sell it and buy two swimming pools and a domed stadium."

"How do you know?"

"My dad's an antiques dealer. He knows all about that stuff."

"My dad's a colonel in the Marine Corps." Snowy growled, as if I had challenged him to a fight.

"Okay," I said gently. Snowy looked angry. I waited for him to say something, but he didn't, so I went on. "Well, I just chipped a little off the back of it with my knife. The vase chip matches these. They're both baked clay. Snowy, somewhere in that cave are remains of glazed pottery."

"But where did you find the four little chips? When? Last night on your socks?"

"That's the thing of it. There was nothing on last night's socks. I checked them carefully before we left the cave. I would have seen these bits right away. They're a different color from the sand. I found them when I washed my hands and they fell off in the sink."

Snowy blindfolded me. We began our trek.

"What did you do before you washed your hands?"

"Took off my clothes. Threw 'em in the laundry pile. Listen, nothing could have stuck to my clothes. Only my socks, and my socks were clean. Just sand. I shook them out. There wasn't anything."

"Go over it again."

I let out an impatient sigh. "Okay. I took off my socks. Right? Then my shirt. Covered with mud from the tunnel. Then my pants. That's it."

"And turned out the pockets like a good boy?" asked Snowy.

"What? Sure. Wait a minute . . . pockets . . . "

"Was that the last thing you did before you washed your hands? Turned out the pockets of your pants?"

"Yes! Damn!" I said. "Except for another pair of socks . . . I took them out of my parka pockets. The socks from the first day across the river. They were frozen, and I didn't put them on again. Snowy, they came from somewhere in our very first squares. We didn't walk long that day. I remember about where we were."

"We're on our way, Barney!" Snowy said. I could hear the smile in his voice.

We plowed through our original squares for nearly an hour and a half. By that time we had piled up a dozen sand mountains as high as our knees.

"Look at that," said Snowy, panting and exhausted. "We've thrown sand over where we might want to dig next. How do we get the stupid piles out of the way?"

Worse, every hole filled in as quickly as we dug it. The swiftly collapsing sides kept slipping back into the pits. "Another complete loss!" Snowy grumbled, throwing his trowel away. "We should have brought shovels."

I was about to suggest that next time he should order an Army Corps of Engineers bulldozer from the back pages of *Soldier of Fortune* when the tip of my trowel touched something hard at the very bottom of the hole. "At least it's ground, if nothing else. The sand can't go down forever," I muttered.

Then we both dug fast and deep. "My knees are freezing," said Snowy. We realized that to get any deeper, we'd have to dig very wide around where we wanted to go, to keep the sandy sides from falling in on themselves.

We cleared away as much sand as we could. Then we started pushing back the huge mound that lay all around us. I stopped with the trowel, lay on my belly, and felt with my fingers. It was just possible as the hole was the depth of my outstretched arm. I pulled my pocketknife from my jeans and, stomach pressed into the frigid sand, I jabbed the blade into the bottom of the pit. I wriggled my hand, working the point deeper into the sand.

"What is it? A dirt bottom? Clay? What do you feel?" Snowy asked.

"Wait a sec. Stone, it seems like."

"Well, the whole cave's made of rock," said Snowy. "Don't expect too much. It's probably just the floor of the cave."

"Damn it. I wish I did have a shovel." Sand began trickling back into the opening.

"We'll never make a dent in all this," said Snowy. "It may be just three feet deep, but you might as well try to move the Sahara."

I didn't answer. I forced my hand down as far as it would go. Then I groped around in the icy sleeve of sand and slid my fingertip back and forth, to make sure I was right, and yanked out my arm. The entire hole caved in as if it had never been dug.

"What did you find?" Snowy asked.

"Just stone. But there's something different about it."

"What?"

"It's not the same bumpy stone that's in the rest of the cave. It's as smooth as marble. But the funny thing is, there's a crack in it."

"So?"

"Well, the crack felt like a straight line. As if it was cut against a ruler. You know? Not some zigzag crack like you find anywhere. Maybe I'm crazy. Maybe it's nothing."

Snowy dived headlong into the sand. He stuck his hand down as far as it would go, but his arm was too short to hit bottom. He took it out, and we watched the hole fill right up again. "Still, we've got something to dig for now," he said. "Next time we'll bring shovels. And blankets too, to kneel on."

"Next week," I said gloomily, "is Christmas vacation. You'll be here, I guess. Exploring away."

Snowy set his trowel down and brushed off his hands. "I'm supposed to go to my mother," he said slowly.

"Where?" I asked.

"Out of the country," he answered. "But I can always tell her I'm going to my uncle."

"Where's he?" I asked.

"I could tell my uncle, of course, that I'm going to mother's. Neither of them would know, you see.

They haven't spoken to each other in years. So they won't check. I'll stay here," he said, satisfied with this arrangement. "How about you?"

"I'm spending Christmas Day in Denver with my dad. On the twenty-sixth I'm supposed to go on to Aspen, where my cousins are skiing. My dad can't ski because of his back, so he's flying straight on to Europe for a big auction in London. Months ago, when my dad arranged this, he told me to bring a friend for two weeks of skiing. I was going to ask Rudy or Danny. Isn't that a laugh! I think I still have to go skiing, though. I mean, my dad won't be home, and there's no place else for me to go."

Snowy messed with some more sand, building a little castle. "I thought you hurt *your* back," he said with a bland smile.

I grinned back broadly. "I forgot about that," I said. "It's not as if I'd disappoint anyone if I didn't go skiing. My cousins are all older than I am. They think I'm just a cute little kid." I cleared my throat. "Would the Finneys take me in too?" I asked.

"I'll see what they say. I'll drop a note in your box."

CHAPTER EIGHT)

On the second night after Christmas the Finneys were polite but frosty. Finney himself watched me as if from a great height. I did the dishes, I brought in firewood, and I even walked the dog. I combed my hair three times an evening, made sure not to put my elbows on the table, and stood up like a jack-in-the-box when Dr. Dorothy came in the room.

On the fourth night I offered to strip and refinish a Georgian drum table. Finney said I should stop acting like a valet, as he was not General Zia. Then he showed me his wooden leg.

"It's beautiful!" I blurted out before I thought about what to say.

Finney chuckled proudly. He'd pulled his pants leg up to the knee to display it. The leg was made of laminate—slivers of different-colored woods cemented together. They made as nice a calf, ankle, and foot as any cabinetmaker's prize piece. "I had it done by a ship's carpenter I know," said Finney. "Over my dead body would the doctors make me wear some ugly thing from a drugstore that sells trusses to people at death's door. I lemon-oil it once a week. Polish it with a chamois cloth."

"Does it come off?" I asked.

"Sure it does," Finney answered, "but if I took it off to show you, Dorothy'd have my head. She thinks it's vulgar."

Dr. Dorothy and Snowy had disappeared these two nights, after the supper dishes were cleared, into her enormous laboratory at the back of the house. There Dr. Dorothy bred and trained guinea pigs for Harvard University. There were mazes and levers and colored lights and bells for all kinds of intelligence tests. She owned at least fifty pigs. They all had names. There were several white rats too, without names. They interested me on a level with the economy of Latvia.

Snowy's Christmas present from the Finneys was a white-and-brown guinea pig he called Rosie. At the Finneys' house Snowy had gone nowhere without Rosie. She sat in her grapefruit carton at the dinner table while we ate, chewing her lettuce. She slept in her box by Snowy's bed and next to the tub when he took a shower. She curled contentedly in his lap, gently nibbling his caressing fingers wherever else he was.

"So did you have a nice Christmas, Pennimen?" asked Finney, helping himself to a macaroon and settling back in his chair by the fire.

"Yes. My dad and I had Christmas dinner at a big hotel in Denver. We had goose. I'd never eaten it before."

"Your father called here, you know. Just to make sure everything was on the up and up." Finney worried one of his molars with a metal toothpick. "He wants you to leave Winchester. He thinks Mr. Silks has treated you unfairly, and he thinks Rudy and the boys will hurt you one day."

"I know he thinks that. It's all we talked about, Christmas. I told him I want to stay."

"I agree with your father. I also think Silks may find a way to keep you out of Hotchkiss even if you do nothing wrong from here on. From what I hear, Mr. Silks seems to think you are a ringleader and a troublemaker. Why do you want to stay here, Pennimen?"

"I just do."

"A better answer, please."

"The school Dad wants to send me to is Monterey

Academy in California. It's not . . . like Winchester."

"I know of the school. It has a certain reputation."

I waited to see what kind of reputation, but Finney seemed to take my answer for what it was and did not blast Monterey out of the water. He clucked for his collie.

Like a shadow unfolding, the dog crept out from under her table and, slicing me with her eyes, put her muzzle on his good knee. "I've had boys do bad things, Pennimen," Finney said, staring at the fire and petting the dog. "In the old days here at Winchester new boys were made to drink ink by the seniors. Then they had to piss blue in front of everyone. Boys have run cheating rings before, they have stolen the way you did, and sneaked in liquor and played pranks just the way you did. Most of those boys grew up to be decent men. But no boy I've ever had in thirty years would have attacked my dog like young Mr. Sader and his friends." Finney shook his head. "They'll try to get you, Pennimen. You should listen to your dad. Go to Monterey. Go away from here. You'll make your way back into a good school the following year."

I traced the pattern of the Persian carpet with a poker and tried to think of something to say. The fire hissed and popped. The collie purred, much like a cat. In Finney's intelligent eyes the orange reflection of the flames danced. "It's the cave, isn't it, Pennimen?" Finney asked.

I nodded.

"Tell me what you've found."

"I can't. I promised Snowy. If I say anything, he'll never take me back there."

"You mean you don't know where this bloody cave is? I thought you were down there every day working like an Egyptian hod carrier!"

"I am. But Snowy blindfolds me and walks me in circles first, so I don't know where the entrance is."

Finney digested this and another macaroon for a minute. "Poor Cobb," he muttered at last. "Doesn't trust a soul. He's had a tough life. I expect you know about it."

I wanted to know more, so I said casually, "His mom's living in a foreign country?"

Finney gave the collie a macaroon. "His mother . . . travels," he said. "The father was a career Army man, I think. Stationed in the East somewhere. Been missing seven years. Cobb thinks he's alive and working secretly for the CIA. The Army says he's dead. Cobb has an uncle who brought him here. Dorothy and I have taken him in, you know. Cobb needs a home. He came to Dorothy and me because he was petrified of your former friends." Finney said this with a half smile and a direct look in my eyes.

"I wish you were back as headmaster, Mr. Finney," I said.

"Do you mean that, Pennimen? I punished you rather hard, as I remember."

"I deserved it."

"Do you mean that too?" His eyebrows rose, and I could feel the human lie detector again.

I nodded, catching his gaze.

"I'm too old to get another job as headmaster, you know," he said sadly. "They want young blood out there. Not old academic fools like me."

Sleet bristled against the windows, and the wind wailed like a far-off horn. I could feel the sadness in Finney, as I sometimes felt it across the room when my father was thinking of my mother. "Mr. Finney?"

"Yes, Pennimen."

"What do you suppose will happen to those boys? Especially Rudy and Danny? What kind of men will they grow up to be?"

"Ha ha ha ha," Finney laughed sourly.

I waited. There was no answer but the tumbling of a log onto the hearth. Then, quite suddenly, Mr. Finney spat into the fire.

CHAPTER NINE)

Snowy and I had nearly two weeks of full days. We began at seven in the morning and left in the evening, when the bats flew out at five thirty through their roof window. It took two hours of digging with large spades to get to the bottom of our hole without the sand caving in. This time we made it big enough for both of us to get into. We created another waste mountain in doing this and promised each other we'd take turns hauling it away.

At the very bottom was the surface I'd felt with the tips of my fingers.

I straddled it and shone the flashlight down on it. There below me, the size of a domino, was a white stone block. It had been cut in a perfect rectangle. Beyond it was another, just the same, and three more.

Snowy slipped opposite me into the hole. He just fit. "My God!" we both said together, for the stones had all been perfectly chiseled and set in the soft clay around them.

"Somebody *made* this, Barney!" crowed Snowy. "Somebody made this just the way they made the steps. There *is* more here! There *is*!"

"What do you think it is?" I asked.

"I don't know. Looks something like a pathway," said Snowy.

"I think so too." I brushed it cleaner and cleaner. "Leading to the river. And the other way leading back into the cave."

"Which way do we go?" he asked.

"Back, I think. If the road goes anywhere, it would be away from the river."

Snowy wiped his sweaty face with his forearm. "Wait," he said. "The steps on the other side of the river? They're directly opposite this road. Maybe nothing's here and it's all on the other side?"

All, I thought. All. What was *all* going to be? A village? One little play hut? Was this a joke? Or a model? "Snowy," I said, "you know what?"

"What?"

"Suppose we're looking at something that no one has seen or touched since before the birth of Christ. Maybe since the Greeks or Noah's ark. How do we . . . not wreck it by mistake?"

"Which way, Barney?" said Snowy, unimpressed.

"Back," I insisted. "Back into the cave on this side of the river. . . . Oh, no. Dammit," I added. "Look what we've done. Just where we want to dig we've covered over the surface with the sand we've cleared from this hole."

Snowy said nothing. He gazed at the sand mountain unhappily. He and I knew it would take a lot of work to get rid of it. And then what? Supposing we threw all that sand on top of another place that turned out to be promising? How were we going to deal with all the sand we dug up?

"We have to think about how to do this better," said Snowy. "If only there was a way . . . you know, when they send divers down to look at shipwrecks, they don't just dump them overboard in the middle of the ocean. I've watched it on TV. They have a sonar or something that they beam at the bottom to see if anything's down there."

"But we don't have a sonar or a periscope camera, and we don't have a scientist to tell us what to do," I said.

"Well, supposing we took something. I don't know, like a broom handle. And we attached the blade of your pocketknife to the end of it."

"A boathook. Finney's got one in his garage.

Under all those old tires. It's heavy and long. The tip is rounded, but I can file it to a point."

We called them "soundings" after the sonar on the ships. Altogether we made seventeen before we began to dig again.

"We still have to do something with the sand we dig up," Snowy reminded me. "So as not to just throw it on top of another diggable place."

"Put it in the river?"

"Supposing that floods the river, and the water ruins all our digging?"

"Will it?"

"I don't know. We'll just have to risk it."

"Okay. Once we find something really big, we dig in shifts. Half an hour digging, half an hour hauling sand away, then switch."

"That'll double the time it takes to find anything," said Snowy.

"We could hire high school kids from Greenfield," I said.

Snowy was furious. "Don't ever make jokes about bringing anybody else here," he warned me. "You hear me, Barney? This is my cave. My cave."

"Come on," I answered, but I knew I'd never say anything like that again.

By this time Snowy had stolen all the remaining site stakes from the pool digging company, which had stopped work because of the frozen ground. We had placed stick markers in those soundings that had stone bottoms. There were four. The rest of the time the boathook had hit soft, dense clay.

"I wish we had a periscope with a light," I moaned. "I wish we had an electric shovel, and I wish the cave were at least fifty degrees."

"You giving up?"

"Of course not. I can wish, can't I?"

"Okay. Let's go. We've got four sites with stone."

"But which one?" I said. "Wait a minute. Let's do something smart for a change. Let's take each of the soundings with stone underneath and make lots more soundings around it to see if we can find some other stuff that feels like something else. Otherwise we might just hit the road and more road."

My imagination was flying. I couldn't keep it from what I knew were idiot ideas. Finally I rested on the boathook after several jabs and asked point-blank, "Where did you read that story about the pygmies on the Pacific island, Snowy?" I was hoping, just hoping that he might say *National Geographic* or *The New York Times.*

"I don't remember," he answered. "But it's true."

"How do you know it's true?"

"My father told me," he said solemnly.

I pried him a little. "Did your dad . . . did he interview the guy who saw the—"

"My father does secret work for the government," Snowy snapped. "I'm not supposed to discuss it."

We made more soundings. And all the while I thought about the men, fuzzy and distant, that Snowy had circled with question marks in the *Soldier of Fortunes*. Was he looking for his dad among those strange men? Could his father actually be in one of those pictures?

"Here! Here! Here!" he shouted suddenly, after taking the boathook and turning it around the way a surgeon might explore with a scalpel—gently, lightly as a fly.

"What have you got? Another stone? What?" I asked.

"It's a thing," Snowy answered.

We scrabbled and gouged for what seemed six hours but turned out to be two. And then we stood over them.

"Jackpot!" said Snowy.

For a few seconds neither Snowy nor I moved. The squashed sand beneath our knees trickled stubbornly back down into the pit. I listened to the silence, broken only by the eternal dripping of the ceiling and the low roar of the underground river.

In the center of our little pit the stone roadway widened into a perfectly paved circle, then continued off into the cave. But at the far side of the circle sat two glistening black figures.

They were about the size of jackrabbits. Heads of men, helmeted, with curly beards jutting out, had been carved onto the bodies of curled-up serpents. Each had a fiercely opened cape around his head and shoulders. Each had a squared-off beard and savage, staring eyes.

Later I drew one, exactly as we first saw him, sitting on a bed of sandy clay in the flickering light of our lantern.

Snowy and I both reached out at the same instant, hands trembling, and our eyes bugging out like kids' in a toy store. We touched them. Then both of us went into a frantic dive action, squirming ourselves down to ground level, shining the light on every detail, caressing them as if they were alive.

"They're sunk way into the ground," said Snowy. "Can't move 'em."

"What are they made of?" I asked. "It looks like a kind of black glass."

"I don't know. I don't know, but what are they? What do they mean?"

"Some kind of . . . well, gods or mythical demons. Some kind of guards? Beginning of something? A gateway! Maybe this part of the road leads to where the people lived who made these things. It almost looks as if they were put here to mark the road and scare people."

"Scare people?"

"Well, say this is a scale model of some Indian civilization. Look at the size of the river steps. In scale that would make a person about six, eight inches tall. Okay? These things are over a foot and a half tall. They'd be terrifying full size, three times the height of a man. I wonder where the real thing would be?" I said.

"The real thing?" Snowy asked.

"The real road. The real statues. The real Indian civilization that this is a scale model of."

"Barney," said Snowy, "this is the real thing. This is no scale model."

"How do you know so much?"

Snowy shrugged absentmindedly. I knew he was thinking about Pacific pygmies. Meantime he stared, calculating, from one to another of the man-serpents. "This is the way we go, Barney," he said, pointing between them to the road that led into a bank of sand.

We said nothing to Finney that night or the next two. I was exhausted and fell into bed each night around seven. Snowy, who never talked much about the cave anyway, was entirely caught up in the birth of twelve new guinea pigs. We began getting up at six and would gulp down four eggs, toast, a quart of milk and orange juice between us, and pack an equally big lunch. Dr. Dorothy said she felt as if she were feeding two forest rangers.

We dug for four full days, finding nothing but more road. I paced off the distance we'd covered. Twenty-one yards. Little white brick followed little white brick. The only other things we came across were some odd black holes in the clay lining the pathway. We called them splash holes because they looked as if they were made by spilling molten metal into the ground. We dug up several, but the holes were empty. Nonetheless I drew a few pictures of them.

"Supposing the dumb road goes for a mile," I groaned, leaning on my shovel after one tough hour of digging.

"Then we dig for a mile," said Snowy. "Wait. What's that?"

"What's what?"

"Little white thing by the side of the road there. Looks like a tiny gravestone."

"I think it's a marker of some kind, maybe. You don't put a grave by the side of the road. . . . Hey, Snowy, I have an idea."

"What?"

"My dad . . . " I stopped to catch my breath, hunkering down on the sand. "My dad has some stone rubbings. From a cathedral in England. People rub 'em on paper right off the grave lids. You got the pencil and paper?"

"Somewhere," said Snowy, climbing carefully out so as not to disturb our trench, which now measured about a foot and a half in width at the bottom, widening to six feet at the top.

When we got back to the stable in the failing

winter light and Snowy had removed my blindfold, we had a good look at my rubbing. It was on lined paper from a notebook, and the pencil was not dark enough to make it pretty, but this is what was carved on the marker.

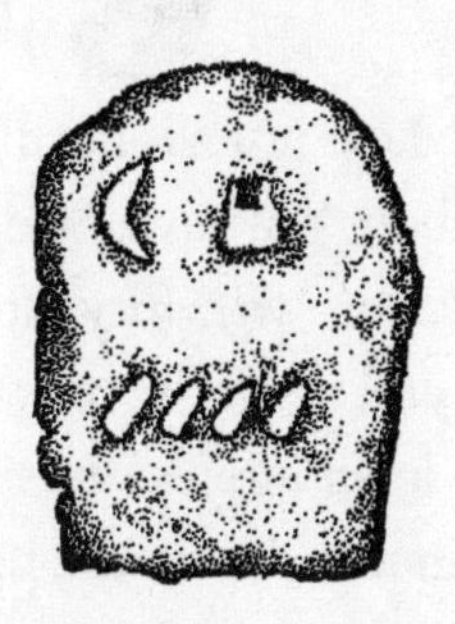

"It looks like a moon shape," said Snowy. "Quarter moon. Then there's the other odd shape and then four little darts."

"We'll never figure it out."

"We might if we find more writing," said Snowy. "It may be an Indian language."

We walked slowly back to the Finneys'. "Why don't we show it to the old man?" I asked.

"You show it to Finney and you'll never see the cave again," said Snowy.

"Oh, come off it. Why not? You showed him the bone, didn't you?"

"But this writing is important stuff. If we show it

to Finney, he'll want to give it to some language expert."

"Look, Snowy," I grumbled, getting angry, "where would you be without me? Huh? Nowhere. You'd be sitting in your damn cave fooling around with a petunia trowel."

Snowy answered me just as angrily. "We let other people find out about the cave," he said, "and in a month it'll be overrun with fifty clowns from Harvard. It's my cave and it's going to stay my cave!"

We walked on in an unpleasant silence. I broke it after about ten minutes. "Who the hell do you think made that stuff?" I asked. "And please don't tell me about a bunch of pygmies the size of a G.I. Joe doll."

Snowy shrugged and eyed the fast-setting sun in front of us. "In this part of the world it's got to be Indians," he said softly, "but somehow it doesn't look Indian."

"How much do you know about Indians?" I asked.

"Not much. The usual moccasin and birch bark canoe kind of thing."

"Save me a trip to the library, Snowy," I said.

Grudgingly he looked over at me.

"Let me ask Finney if he knows anything about Indian tribes, particularly from around here." I went on. "Okay? Look, both of us have exam week coming up at the end of the month. It'll take days to find out what Finney could tell us in a few minutes."

Snowy struggled silently for a few minutes. "Only if you make him promise not to tell. And I'll be listening from the lab to everything you say, even with the door closed and the dehumidifier on," he added sulkily.

"Snowy, how come you don't trust anybody? Even me? Even the Finneys? I'm your buddy, Snowy. I mean that."

Snowy said nothing. Peter Mellor was dead right about the rubber ice cube tray. That's exactly what Snowy was. A rubber ice cube tray.

"Rosie's going to have babies," he announced suddenly. "Dr. Dorothy's going to breed her to the big fat black-and-tan pig, Charles. I get to keep one of the babies if I want."

This little trinket of information touched me in the heart. Snowy strode on beside me over the ice-pocked field. He held his head high, looking at the drab clouds and sniffing from cold now and then.

My imagination had hopped far away to the sands of the cave and the people who had built the white stone road, who had carved the imposing man-serpent statues, and who had written a message on a piece of marble no bigger than my thumb.

CHAPTER TEN)

Don't mind me, Pennimen," said Finney. As usual he'd settled himself into his armchair in front of the fire. He rubbed the side of his face deeply with his fingers and explained he was having an attack of neuralgia. My father did the same thing when he was thinking of income tax, or when he was afraid he'd bought a fake.

I sat in the opposite chair, drawing one of the black man-serpents in pencil. Later I finished it in ink.

A quiet fifteen minutes passed. Finney massaged. I drew.

"I understand you're quite an artist," he said. "Are you doing a cartoon of me, by any chance?"

"No," I said. "This is something different. We've found something." I glanced up anxiously toward the lab, where Snowy and Dr. Dorothy were fussing around. At dinner they'd said they were going to conclude a series of tests on sound perception in two different strains of guinea pigs. I wanted to talk to Finney alone because I was afraid, no matter what I said, it would go too far for Snowy. "We've found three or four things, actually," I added.

"Have you?" asked Finney gently, but his eyes began to light up.

"Do you know much about the Indians who were here long ago, Mr. Finney?"

I kept sketching as he talked. He lit his pipe and stopped working at the side of his head. "A bit," he said. "Wampanoags, some Mohicans from the north. None of the more famous tribes like the Apaches or the Mohawks. These were peaceful people. They were hunters. They grew some corn, and they were set upon and lost everything to our white ancestors. That was a great shame because they were far ahead of our ancestors in some ways. They were not greedy, and they did not make war. It was the end of them. Our ancestors were greedy, and they did make war, and that will be the end of us. What an irony!"

"Did they write in symbols?"

"No. They did some painting. Animals on hides. But no native North Americans had any written language whatsoever. They didn't need it," said

Finney, puffing great fumes of smoke straight upward.

"Need it?"

"They didn't trade. That's why writing started. Did you know that?"

"No." I stopped drawing.

"The earliest bits of writing ever found are bills, receipts, and orders. If people trade things and pay for things, they have to keep records. I've seen clay tablets dating back to three thousand years before Christ. You know what they are? Arguments between a copper merchant in Sumeria and some ship's captain who delivered a load of rotten grain."

"I didn't know that."

"Sure. After people learned to keep accounts, then they started writing history and decorating tombs with messages about gods and kings and so forth. But it all started with business. Money. The original occupants of this continent did not trade in volume, in other words run businesses like the Egyptians or the Greeks. They never started any written languages whatsoever, although some Missouri Mound Builders came very close. Pennimen, what—"

"How about stone carving?" I asked.

"Nope. Why should they? There have always been so many forests around this part of the world.

Much easier to carve wood. You find stone carving in other civilizations. Not here."

"Never? No tribe? Ever? Were there different Indians before the Wampanoags?"

"Not that I know of. Now it's my turn to ask questions, Pennimen. What have you found?"

But I kept going. "Did they have roads?"

"Roads! No! What on earth would they need roads for? They didn't have wheeled vehicles. No regular going from town to town. No towns. Pennimen, what have you found in that cave?"

I showed him the picture of the man-serpent.

"What on earth is this?" he asked.

"There are two, made of black stone. Nearly two feet tall. They're on a road made from tiny stone blocks cut exactly to fit in perfect rectangles. This is a rubbing from a stone marker next to the road. That's all we've found except for a set of white stone steps leading down to the river, and the bone, of course. We figured . . . we figured that long ago some Indians made a big scale model of a village. Snowy'll kill me for telling you," I added, lowering my voice, "but he did say I could ask a few questions."

Finney looked from my drawing of the statue to the rubbing from the marker and back again. I sat and waited, time prickling me, hoping he wouldn't quash our discovery with some adult explanation that would make perfect sense and wreck the whole joy of it.

"This has nothing to do with Native American history, early, late, or in between. They did not make this. They did not know about roads. And this is a primitive language, hieroglyphics . . . you know what that is?"

I'd had ancient history in sixth grade. "Yes . . . the Egyptian writing."

"Exactly. Picture-symbols. But look at the beard you've drawn here. Did you get it right, you think?"

"That's how it looked."

"This man or god has a curly beard. Every American Indian ever born had hair as straight as a die. Everything about the face, the eye, the nose is wrong. American natives migrated here thousands of years ago from the Orient when the Bering Strait in Alaska was a land bridge. This is not Indian. How big did you say this statue is?"

"A foot and a half high maybe. The stones in the road are about two inches long and the steps maybe half an inch high and two inches wide each."

"Pennimen, what have you found?"

"That's what I'm asking you, Mr. Finney."

"Find more."

CHAPTER ELEVEN

Snowy and I did our best to find more, working hours a day until Christmas vacation was at an end. We bickered about how much I had told Finney. We argued about whether we were digging in a wrong direction again. We tried more random soundings with our boathook, but because the road curved and changed direction, we stuck it down blind and came up empty each time. The road was now more than fifty yards long. The cave went on beyond, infuriatingly smooth and clueless.

When school began in the new year, I had almost no time to dig because of midterm exams. They loomed at the end of January. Unless I did well, all chances of getting into Hotchkiss would be lost. Snowy didn't care about studying.

He made slow progress by himself during the middle two weeks of January. Every evening before he left campus, he reported to me in the library. First he talked about his Rosie. He was teaching Rosie a complicated series of mazes. I wished Rosie a long, long life for Snowy's sake. He tried sounding scientific about Rosie but didn't succeed.

Only after he'd described the little guinea pig would he go on about the cave. More road. Endless white road. Endless splash holes beside the road. He had dug up several more, but there was nothing in the holes and no explanation for their odd splashed shape. I told him to give up and wait until my exams were through and I could help him. He didn't.

I crammed for exams like a biblical scholar. I read *Macbeth* three times through, memorized the Cliff notes, learned by rote the declensions of every Latin noun in our book, and took my list of the atomic weights of the elements to bed with me. The battles of the Civil War raged in my dreams, General Sherman and Stonewall Jackson leapt around on isosceles triangles while I strained to figure the area of overlapping trapezoids.

I was prepared. I was completely prepared to handle anything any of my teachers could throw my way.

Then, the night before exams, Rudy and Danny strolled into my room at nine in the evening.

Rudy jerked his thumb at Peter Mellor. Mellor bounced out of his bed and vanished through the door like a bunny. So much for a roommate.

"Hey, man. How about a deal?" asked Rudy.

"What deal?"

"Class notes. History, Latin, English," said Rudy.

"And science," added Danny. "Just like old times, man!"

"You know something, Barney?" Rudy went on. "We figure Finney and Silks probably threatened to bust your lights out after that thing with the collie. So no hard feelings, okay? We've talked about it and we understand. Sometimes these things happen. We won't bother you again."

"If I give you my class notes?" I asked.

"Yeah. That's all, buddy, then everything's gonna be real sane."

I was tempted to do it, but some spring inside me quivered and gave out. To help them cheat again would be to throw dust in the eyes of some unseen god. That god would surely trip me up. To help them cheat would do other boys out of the best grades. Not to mention the fact that if I were caught, I'd be thrown out and never see east of the Mississippi River again. "I can't," I said.

"Why?" they both asked at once, sitting down on

the end of my bed like two huge doctors.

"If you get caught, guys, that's it. I'm in it as deep as you. I'm on probation. You get caught and Silks'll yank my toenails out."

"Come on, Barney," said Danny. "Greeves is proctoring. He wouldn't know it if the whole class showed up naked."

"Besides," Rudy put in, "you don't use the notes. It's only us. We'll take our chances. No skin off you, you're clean."

"If I do it," I said, "and you guys get hauled in, I'm a part of it, and it'll get out somehow. You'll tell Silks. You'll drag me in, and I'll deserve it. If I do it, I will be part of it. And I'll get thrown out of here without a hope in hell of any other school even looking at me. Come on, guys. The same goes for you. Three swimming pools won't get you off the hook if you get caught, Damascus. Your old man'll set all ten of his Doberman pinschers on you if you don't get into Choate. Forget it."

Danny's eyes began to burn, but he let Rudy talk.

"My butt is my problem," said Rudy. "I'm taking the chance. I've gotta get at least a B plus to keep my scholarship and get into Lawrenceville."

"I swear to God, Barney," said Danny, "you give us the notes, we get caught, we don't tell. Swear."

I laughed. "You think I'd believe that? You think I'd take Swoboda's word for it after he nearly put me in the hospital with his elbow? You really think I'd believe you?" I stood up. "Sorry, guys. I can't do it. I gotta watch out for my own butt."

"You're gonna watch more than your butt if you don't, Barney," said Danny, kneading his big hands.

"Go to hell," I answered him.

"What did you say?" barked Rudy.

"You heard me."

"Oh, boy, did we hear you," Danny whispered.

Mellor crept back into the room a half hour later. He didn't say boo.

I tried to sleep. I kept reasoning with myself that without a decent night's rest I could easily fail Latin and English. I fell asleep sometime before dawn. When I dragged myself out of bed, I glanced, bleary-eyed, at my Latin notes. Hadn't I put them under the English book the night before? I was sure I had because English was the last thing I'd studied. Had someone messed with my notes?

The Latin exam was at eight. I could think about nothing but the warm heaven of bed. Breakfast with three cups of strong tea hadn't woken me up. Every little hair on my body screamed at me that it had been yanked. I waded through a few easy declensions and a Caesar translation as if they were in Bulgarian.

That afternoon English was worse. Lids drooping, I picked over my essay on *Macbeth,* certain I had confused large parts of it with *Arrowsmith* and *Gulliver's Travels.*

Mr. Greeves was everybody's favorite proctor. Stone deaf when he turned his hearing aid off, he was pushing ninety. For half an hour he'd been daydreaming out the window, gazing at one of the big old elms, and looking with love at his collection of bonsai trees along the windowsill.

Greeves was the art teacher. He owned a master's degree in Japanese painting and was fond of telling us about his years spent painting stones in the gardens of Kyoto. My first year at Winchester, when he had still trusted me, he had taken me in hand. He had tried to teach me to draw and to paint, to see in the Japanese way. At that time, if I had done what he asked, I would have been labeled a weirdo, so I didn't. "Why should I?" I asked him. "I'm American. Why should I draw in the Japanese way?"

"Because," Greeves had said, "you are in the country of the blind. And in the country of the blind, the one-eyed man is king!"

I followed the old man's eyes to the winter branches outside the window. I guessed he was imagining them in Japanese watercolor, where they would be beautiful instead of bleak.

He turned from the window and gazed with sleepy pleasure at the boys' bowed heads. A roomful of cramped bodies wrote feverishly in front of his desk. Then, very suddenly, Mr. Greeves put on his glasses and squinted fixedly at something on the floor, mid-room.

Pass or fail, there was not a syllable more that I could write about *Macbeth.* I picked up my blue book and dropped it on Greeves's blotter. Since no talking was allowed during exams, I scribbled Greeves a note on an empty page, asking for permission to leave. He shook his head and pointed for me to sit down again.

I'd just drifted to sleep, head on my desk, when I heard the snap of a ruler hitting a book in the front of the room. Fifty-three bodies jumped like bees on a griddle.

"Every boy in the room stand and fold his arms in front of him!" Greeves ordered in a froggy voice. Every boy did.

He began in the center aisle. He stalked first up to Rudy and made him kick off his shoes. "Give those things to me," said Greeves. Slowly Rudy pulled out his insoles, covered with blue ink shorthand notes. Greeves pocketed them and went on to Danny.

Rudy looked not at Greeves but directly at me. In his eyes were tears. They began running down his face. He did not bother to brush them away. It was not until Danny and Matt also turned to look at me that I understood.

"Oh, God, no!" I whispered to myself. *They think I went up to Greeves's desk and wrote him a note squealing on them.* All of us were dismissed but the five untouchables.

Silks caught up with me in the dorm. "Take off those boots," he yelled.

"Okay, okay." I put my hands up for a moment and then bent and unlaced the boots. I kicked them in his direction. He stuffed his hands in both and came up with sand.

"Where did you throw the cheat notes, Pennimen?"

"I don't have any cheat notes, Mr. Silks! How could I put cheat notes into laced-up boots, anyway?"

"What shoes were you wearing in the exam? Tell me. Tell me right now where they are."

"I don't own any shoes, Mr. Silks. I have loafers, but they don't fit anymore. You can look in my closet. I was supposed to get new ones over Christmas, but . . ."

Silks held me by the shirt front, his face directly over mine. I could smell the Life Saver in the back of his mouth. "You organized this. Didn't you, Pennimen? All five boys sitting this minute in my office say you taught them chapter and verse how to cheat and gave them the notes. You've been doing it for years. They told me your other six systems too. You're a ringleader. You admitted this yourself in Mr. Finney's office last fall. Now you've done it again."

"Please, Mr. Silks." I struggled against his arm. "They came to my room last night. They asked me for notes and I said no! They stole them while I was asleep. It's the truth!"

"Why didn't you tell me they came and asked you?"

"Because you said never to squeal!"

Silks dropped me. "You have destroyed the careers of five promising boys. You will not get away with this."

He walked off like a twister.

"Then what happened?" asked Finney.

"All five boys told Silks I'd tipped off Greeves they were cheating."

"But you did not tip off Mr. Greeves."

"Are you kidding? I just scribbled a note to Greeves asking if I could leave the exam because I was finished. Tip off Greeves! Mr. Finney, I'm not crazy! I don't want them to kill me! I told Silks to ask Greeves what my note said."

"And what did Mr. Greeves say to Mr. Silks?"

"He'd forgotten about my note. I couldn't find it anywhere in the classroom. In the wastebasket, anywhere. Mr. Finney, you know Mr. Greeves is as old as God. He forgets the boys' names in class. Sometimes I think he's forgotten his own name."

Finney nodded, tapped his pipe stem against his front teeth, and focused his eyes somewhere north of me. He asked, "Why didn't you give them the notes the night before, Pennimen? You did it in the past. They would have been off your back."

"It . . . I didn't want to be that way anymore."

Finney used his pipe tool to free some mud from the side of his shoe. "This is what will happen," he said. "The boys were caught cheating in front of the whole senior class. They will be put on probation for the balance of the year, deprived of honors, team sports, et cetera, et cetera. Rudy, of course, won't have a prayer of getting into Lawrenceville or anywhere else now. His parents will have to pay the balance of his tuition for the year, as he will lose his scholarship.

I know Rudy's father. Rudy's a carbon copy of him. He'll thrash Rudy to within an inch of his life and make him work as a short-order cook twelve hours a day all summer to pay up instead of letting him go to football camp. You'll have to watch out. I think the boys will try to get even with you. Martin Silks will get holy hell from the trustees."

"Silks? Why?"

"Makes the school look bad. His first year as head. The school likes winning championships. They like getting people into places like Lawrenceville on scholarship. It looks good in June when the school publishes all the graduates' choices of schools. Damascus was going to Choate. Hines to Taft. That's down the drain. Nope! The boys will have to be punished because it happened in front of everybody, and the punishment for cheating is clear as day, spelled out in the Winchester student handbook. The trustees can't sweep this one under the rug. They will be furious, and they will take it out on Martin Silks for letting an old geezer like Greeves proctor. They will say that a younger man would have paced up and down the aisles and not let such a thing happen. The trustees are fond of blaming people, and they will blame Silks. Silks is taking it out on you, but he can't touch you. Remember. You admitted this cheating business to me honestly, in my office, last October. You have done your punishment for that and other things. You have a witness to that. Me."

"Mr. Finney, can't you talk to Silks?"

Finney took off his glasses, breathed on them, polished them, and squinted through them. "Silks'd sooner listen to the birds in the trees than to me," he said. "But I can do one small thing for you, Pennimen." He reached into a drawer beside him, fumbled through a pile of junk, and came up with a ring of keys.

"I don't even have to ask you, Pennimen, if you will call your father, report all this, and ask to be transferred to a school in California?"

"No."

"I didn't think so. You still excused from sports?"

"No one seems to notice."

"All right. How do you get to the stables to meet Snowy?"

"I just cut across through the trees near the old building."

"Try a new way." Finney took two keys off the ring. "You know where the music room is? Downstairs in the old building?"

"Yes."

"Okay. Just around the corner from the music room is a door. Before they built the new wing in 1951, that door led to the kitchen. The old kitchen hasn't been used in over thirty years. This key opens the door that leads to it. Go down the stairs into the kitchen. Look to your right. There's a pantry there, also not used, and opening off of it, a very long passageway. Follow the passageway to the end. Go up a set of stairs, and you'll find another door. This second key unlocks that. You will find yourself in the middle of some brick cold frames behind the stable. No one can see where you go once you unlock the first door to the kitchen stairs. Now get back to the campus before lights out. Go on!"

I scuffed over the frosty grass in the quad. Rudy, his eyes full of tears, grew like a fat blister on my mind. I despised Rudy. I hated his guts. But his life would now change for better or for worse because of me, though I wanted no part in Rudy Sader's life. The west dorm, choked over with leafless ivy vines, towered on one side of the quad. Such comforting lights glowed in its windows.

Just then a groan—half pain, half anger—cut into the winter night. So like the collie's cry, but human. Rudy Sader's voice. I felt for him and his stupid wrecked dreams of being a pro quarterback. I don't know why, I just did, and I wanted to tell him, man to man, that I was sorry about what had happened and that I had not turned him in. I sprinted up two flights and knocked on Sader's door.

Very slowly I opened the door. Rudy and his friends froze. The five boys stared at me as if I were a zebra. I imagined hearing the seconds, loud and angry, tick by in the air. Were they all planning to spike my chipped beef on toast with ground glass? Rudy lay on his bed in his underwear, holding a half-empty bottle of Bacardi rum against the pillow. His hair was wildly matted and his face blotched. The room contained a sick, sweet smell.

Rudy spat at me from the bed. I ducked. He got to his feet and spat right in my face. "Wait, Rudy," I said. "I didn't have anything—"

"You filthy little Nazi Jewboy scum," he snarled.

I heard my own voice at a distance, as if it were on a tape. "I came to thay," I said, "I didn't turn you guyth in. I didn't thay anything to Greevth. It wathn't my fault. I'm thorry, Rudy. I—"

Danny grabbed both my arms, kneed me in the small of the back, and doubled me over head first onto Rudy's bed.

"I'll thcream!" I threatened him. "You'll all be

thrown out for good. You can't drink liquor in thchool!"

Somebody dumped a dose of rum on my head. "Yeah? And you'll smell just as drunk as we do, pretty boy." It was Shawn.

"What do we do to him?" asked Brett.

"I wanna kill the bastard," said Rudy. "I got nothing to lose."

"Don't be a jerk. You wanna wind up in the state pen?" Danny said, and through my legs, upside down, I could see him guiding Rudy to the back of the room, gently, as if Rudy were a bobbing prize-fighter. Matt Hines slouched with his back against the door. Brett's body, about a hundred and thirty pounds, held me on the bed. *Pennimen,* I asked myself, *how in hell are you going to get out of this?*

"Open his mouth," said Rudy. "Open his mouth and hold it open."

"No!" I screamed. "What are you going to do? No!"

"Can't leave a mark on him, Sader," Danny warned.

"I'm gonna make him eat a stick of deodorant," said Rudy. "You keep swallowing, Pennimen, or I'll push it down your throat anyway."

I clenched my teeth together against the slick

green cylinder as Rudy pressed on my mouth. His rummy breath drifted over the acid perfume of the Old Spice. "Open, Pennimen, or I'll put it somewhere else."

"No!"

"Take his belt off."

Danny reached under my belly for my belt. At that moment I pumped both my legs out like a kangaroo and caught Danny in the nose.

What Danny would have done next I don't know, as there was a sudden racketing on the open window. For a second I thought it was a hailstorm. It was gravel. Bits of it landed on the floor and bed. Someone down in the quad was hurling handfuls of it at the window.

The whole dorm began stirring. Windows were opened. Lights went on. Boys began running out into the quad. The pebbles stopped. A set of footsteps jogged down the hall and stopped at Rudy's door, and a voice yelled something I couldn't make out.

They poured the rum out the window and hid the bottle in a clutch of vines under the outside sill. Brett yelled at the voice in the hallway to run and get some bandages and iodine. "That'll take him fifteen minutes," Brett whispered. They let me go. On my way out Danny bent the middle finger of my right hand farther back than it would bend.

> If you can wait and not be tired by waiting, Or, being lied about, don't deal in lies, Or, being hated, don't give way to hating, And yet don't look too good, nor talk too wise . . .

"Go on," said Silks. He was peering at my swollen hand.

I began the second verse of "If." He glanced at his watch and stopped me there. "Better get that finger taped, Pennimen," he said. "Baseball season starts soon. Since we've lost half our team, we need all the boys we can get."

"Yes, sir. Do you want me anymore, Mr. Silks?"

His eyes, round and piercing, like black moons in a white sky, ran over me, up and down. "*Want* you, Pennimen? I don't want you at all, boy. Not at all. I never did want you. You have destroyed the senior class here. There is nobody I want less than you."

He grasped his blotter by its leather corners. "You systematically taught five of our most promising boys to cheat. You guided innocent boys in your dirty ways. You admitted this last October when you were told that you would not be expelled if you pointed the finger at others. You are no better than a mobster who sings to the police in exchange for immunity. You are no better than an experienced pickpocket who teaches a youngster his skills. You are a communicable disease in this school."

I tried to meet his eyes. They were expressionless and still focused on my finger. "But what do you want me to do, Mr. Silks?" I asked.

"This is what I want you to do, Pennimen," he said softly, running his tongue over his teeth. "I want you to go away."

"Go away?"

"After that disgraceful incident in the fall when you incited the same boys to torture the headmaster's dog, your—"

"But I didn't, Mr. Silks. I didn't."

"You led them in cheating. There is no doubt in my mind that you perversely led them in everything bad you could dream up. At any rate, Pennimen, your father called the school last November. He wanted to withdraw you and send you to another school in California. You apparently refused. Think about it again."

"I don't understand, Mr. Silks."

"Let me put it this way. Since you are no better

than a jailbird who makes a deal with the district attorney, I will be the district attorney and you will be the jailbird. All right? This is my deal with you. You want to enter Hotchkiss next fall, am I right?"

"Yes, Mr. Silks. I was hoping to if I kept my grades up. Mr. Finney said he'd give me a clean record."

"I am headmaster now, not Mr. Finney! Is that clear, boy?"

It was very clear. I nodded and swallowed and tried to look like an injured bird.

"I will also give you a completely clean record at Winchester, Pennimen. But you must choose to transfer immediately, right now! You may go to any boarding school that has an eighth grade—a middle school. From there, given your three-point-nine average and your completely clean record, you will easily get into Hotchkiss next year. That's what you want, isn't it?"

"Well . . . yes."

"Good. Now you're beginning to see the light. Do that, Pennimen. You may call your father now. I will arrange things quickly, and you can be in any prep school in the country by next Monday. Groton, St. Andrew's, Milford . . . If you want, I will personally recommend you to Middlesex. I happen to know the headmaster there well. From any of these schools you can get into Hotchkiss easily. You may even get into Exeter if you like. But only if you do it now, Pennimen."

"But I . . . I . . . "

"If you choose to stay at Winchester, I am afraid it will be my duty as headmaster to write a letter on your Hotchkiss application telling them exactly what I think of you. Then you won't get in. Think about it, Pennimen." Silks slipped the blotter neatly back under the corner pieces where he'd pulled it out. Then he handed me my science exam. "You'll take the rest of your exams sitting in my secretary's office, away from all the other boys. Believe me, Pennimen, she'll watch you like a hawk."

"Greeves knows they were drinking," said Snowy.

"What?"

Snowy leaned on his shovel handle to rest. "Finney and Dr. Dorothy were talking about it at breakfast," he said.

"Well, what happened?" Using my shirt as a sling, I stuffed my left hand inside between two of the buttons and let it rest. That noon the same doctor who'd diagnosed my back spasm had encased my middle finger in a big metal and tape device. The finger throbbed like a toothache. The knuckle had been dislocated.

"After Danny let you go, some boy went running down to Greeves to get iodine and bandages, of all things."

"I know. He knocked on the door. Matt Hines told him to bring iodine. Just to lose him while they got rid of me and the rum."

"Yeah. Well, the boy went to Greeves, and Greeves came upstairs. First time he's climbed the stairs all year. He smelled the rum. Rudy tried to fake Greeves out that he'd cut himself and needed a bandage. Greeves wasn't fooled. Greeves called Silks, and Silks blew up." Snowy began to shovel the road again.

"Why didn't Silks throw them out? It's right in the handbook you get expelled if you're caught drinking."

"That's the thing of it. You see? Silks is already under the gun because he allowed Greeves to proctor an exam where five boys were caught cheating. That looks bad on his record as headmaster in his first year."

"I know. Finney told me that."

"Well, if it gets out that the boys were drinking on campus, it'll hit the local papers. It'll cause a big mess for Silks. The board of trustees will have a clean sweep and get rid of Silks, Greeves, everybody. Winchester's always had this super image of being a clean school. They want to keep that image. They don't want stuff in the papers. Next thing they'll be scared someone will find cocaine or pot in somebody's gym locker, and the whole thing'll get into *The New York Times.* This happened to some other big deal prep school a couple of years ago, and enrollment went down, contributions stopped, parents went nuts, Finney says. Silks will do anything to keep Winchester quiet. He can shut up Greeves. No one'll listen to Mr. Greeves anyway because he's deaf and old and can't remember what year it is. The thing of it is, Silks can't shut you up."

"What?"

"That's what Finney says. You give Silks nightmares. He thinks you'll report the boys for drinking. This time, next time, it doesn't matter. He thinks you'll do the boys, his job, and the school in. He wants you out of here."

"But how did he know I was even in Rudy's room? No one saw me."

"Barney," said Snowy, "all he had to do was look at your finger."

We dug on. The road wound, curved, but otherwise never changed. Snowy was unusually quiet. Finally, when we took a chocolate-bar break, he hung his head and, emptying sand from his socks, said, "So I guess you'll be leaving?"

I didn't answer.

"I guess you have to, don't you? I mean your dad'll make you do it." Snowy had gotten sand in his chocolate and took a new one out of his pocket, unwrapping the foil slowly. "Besides, if you stay, they'll get you. Next time it'll be your neck instead of your finger."

"Snowy?"

"What?"

"Did you follow me home last night and throw the stones at Rudy's window?"

Snowy munched carefully on his chocolate. He didn't like the nuts in it and bit around them carefully. Then he tossed the nuts over his shoulder.

"Snowy, you did, didn't you?"

"I figured they'd be waiting for you in the bushes," he said. "I never thought you'd be jerk enough to go up to Rudy's room."

"Thanks, Snowy. You saved me."

He brushed his hands on his pants and began to dig again.

"Did they see you out the window?" I asked him.

Snowy shrugged, and I knew they had. "Barney," he said, "look at the sand. Look at the color of the sand."

CHAPTER TWELVE)

"Is this an untapped line?"

"Dad, I'm calling from Mr. Finney's house. Of course it's untapped!"

"That tinhorn Silks isn't listening in?"

"No, Dad."

"Well, I'm flying into Boston day after tomorrow. Get your things together. There's a train from Greenfield at eleven in the morning. I'll meet it at North Station."

"Dad," I said, voice cracking, "I'm not . . . I'm not leaving Winchester."

"Barney, don't even open your mouth to me about—"

"I'm going to stay on. I will not leave."

"Yes, you will, Barney. Oh, yes, you will. I say you'll leave, and you have no choice. If you think for one minute—"

"Dad," I interrupted. I knew exactly where my

father was sitting. On the kitchen counter, boots dangling against the lower cupboard where we kept rice and cereal. I could see the veins sticking out in his neck and pumping away in his temples. I could hear his face get hot and red. "Dad, listen—"

"You listen, Barney. You listen up and listen hard. I have paid good money, over ten thousand bucks a year, to be exact, to give you a decent education. There is no way you can come back here to Lantry and go to high school twenty miles away in Red Arrow. Even if you did, I have to travel all year long. Where are you going to live? With your Uncle Edward? Huh? You want to live with Uncle Edward and worry about his hernia all night long for him? Number three. Your former friend Rudy and his gang are going to take care of you but good. I will not let you spend one more day on a campus with five weasel-brained lumpkins who want to break your neck. Silks said he would not be responsible for any accidents.

"That brings me to Martin Silks. He is the lowest, most disgusting worm I've ever run into. But he's offered us an out. He says he'll give you a twenty-four-carat-gold ticket into any school in the country if you'll leave now. You're going to St. Andrews, Barney. You have been entered and accepted. Are you listening to me?"

"Yes, Dad."

"Do you know what St. Andrew's is?"

"A big deal preppy school in Rhode Island," I answered.

"Yes, Barney. One of the best schools in the United States. You can finish out eighth grade there and continue in their upper school if you want. Or you can transfer to Hotchkiss from St. Andrew's in September. You will under no circumstances come back here or stay on at Winchester. The decision has been made, Barney."

"Dad, I won't go."

"You do not have that option, son."

"Dad, it's my life. And I won't go."

"Barney, why are you acting like a moron? A flea-brain?"

"If you'll listen, I'll tell you, Dad."

"I will listen to nothing, son, because I am thirty years older than you are. You are going to listen to me. You are going to meet me at North Station in Boston in forty-eight hours. I am taking you to Rhode Island myself."

"I won't show up, Dad."

"Then I will come to Winchester."

"You won't find me, Dad."

I heard Dad sigh at the other end of the line. I wished he were in the room. I wanted to hug him tight around his legs, around his rough old jeans, and climb up into his lap as I'd done when I was a little boy. "You give me one good reason, son. And it better be very, very good."

"I don't know if it's good. But it's why, anyway."

"Get it out of your system."

I swallowed my insides, which had bobbed up to mouth level. "Dad, I've done some pretty stupid, rotten things my first years here."

"Okay. Now you have to pay for it. You're getting off cheap."

"No, Dad. I haven't done anything wrong to cause all this mess. Mr. Silks is trying to punish me when I'm innocent."

"That's why you're getting away from that son of a—"

"No, Dad. That's why I'm staying."

"What the hell do you mean by that?"

"Mr. Silks is trying to bribe me with St. Andrew's, Dad. It's dirty. I won't buy it."

A long, long silence answered this. Could I actually hear the mountain wind booming two thousand miles away in the telephone wire? After a while my father cleared his throat. He said, "Of all the reasons in heaven and earth, Barney, why did you have to pick that one?"

"You're shaking," said Finney.

"I guess I am."

"You handled that well, Pennimen."

"Thank you, Mr. Finney."

"You're going to stay on, then? Here at Winchester?"

"I'm going to try."

"Pennimen, *why did you go to Rudy Sader's room?*"

The logs in the fireplace had fallen down on themselves. I made a neat new pile on top of them and poked them till they burned nicely.

"*Why,* Pennimen?"

"I don't know," I said, throwing the tongs on the bricks of the hearth. "I'm an idiot. That's why. I guess it ripped me up to hear him cry out."

Finney uncrossed his legs, lifting the trouser off the lower good one with both hands. On his lap were my drawings of what we had found in the cave that afternoon. His eyes buttoned on mine. "Is it the cave, Pennimen, that's keeping you here? If Silks writes his letter destroying your record for Hotchkiss, that's a big price to pay. The only place that'll take you is military school. Silks will see to that. You could get out of this mess tomorrow and never have to look back."

"I would look back."

"At the cave?"

"At Snowy."

"Snowy?"

"Rudy and Danny'll go after Snowy now," I said. "If I left Winchester, I wouldn't sleep at night thinking of what they might do to him."

Finney inclined his head to the side. He smiled to himself, not to me. I tried to see through his eyes into his mind, but whatever was going on there was very private. He grasped his pants crease and relifted the bad leg over the good one. "Tell me again about this afternoon," he said, looking at the drawings in his lap. "These things, what you called splash holes, lining the road? They look like patterns from a psychological test. What are they?"

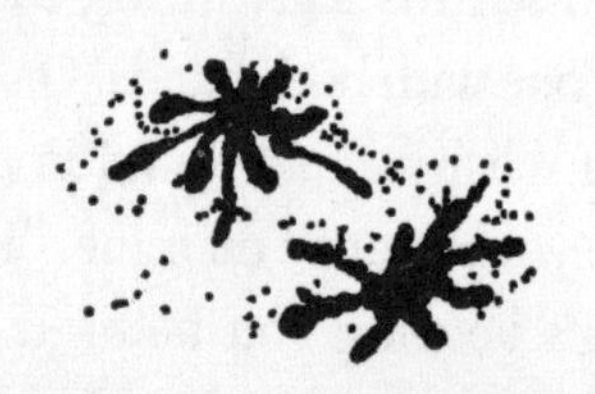

"Well, I don't know what to call them. They're about as big around as . . . as an ink bottle. It's as if someone threw red-hot liquid metal on the ground and it splashed and burned through in a blobby pattern. But there's nothing inside them."

Finney frowned. "Hollow?" he asked.

"Yes, as if something was in them once."

"Cobb! Get in here!" Finney brayed suddenly.

It took Snowy his usual long time to do anything he was asked. Finally he shuffled in and sat down at Finney's feet. Cuddled in Snowy's hands was Rosie, eyes bright, little nose quivering. He fed Rosie a cherry tomato.

"Cobb," said Finney brightly, "will you do us the honor of talking about these little black holes in the ground in that very private cave of yours?"

"Let Barney talk about them," Snowy answered, sniffing.

Finney shook his head. "Okay." He held up both hands. "You're afraid of the curse of the tomb of the cave people."

"It's not funny," said Snowy. "Every single person who dug up King Tut's tomb in Egypt died soon after."

Oh, no, I thought. I'd read that story in one of

Snowy's *Soldier of Fortunes* three weeks before. It was entitled "Poisoned in the Pyramids," and it was all jazzed up with a French Foreign Legion squadron that inhaled four-thousand-year-old mustard gas.

"This isn't a tomb," said Finney. "It's something else. And for your information, Cobb, the fellow who discovered Troy lived to a ripe old age. So did the people who dug up ancient Assyria, who found Easter Island and the cave paintings at Lascaux. So there."

"It's my cave," said Snowy.

"Yes, I know, Cobb. And I am going to ask you to do something special in your cave, all right?"

"What?"

"What you boys call splash holes. I want you to fill a couple of them with plaster of paris. Let it dry. Dig up the whole thing. Bring it back to me."

Snowy gave his glasses a shove up his nose and didn't answer.

"I will tell you something, Cobb," Finney went on. "Every single thing I've seen in Pennimen's pictures could have been made up. Could have been just your imaginations. Except for these." Finney stood, wobbling, and reached for a book. He opened it to a picturc of what looked like a Roman courtyard. "This is Pompeii," he said. "This is a garden two thousand years old, boys. Pear trees, lindens, and crab apples used to grow there. You know how they found that out?"

But Finney didn't have to go any further. On the page were photographs of black holes identical to ours except much larger. "They filled these holes with wax," he explained. "When the wax hardened inside, they dug it up and from the mold of the root were able to identify every tree that grew in that garden. It's possible that something once alive grew in these little holes of yours. Try plaster of paris in them. Now, tell me about this so-called fire pit you found this afternoon, Pennimen."

Snowy picked up Rosie and left the room.

"We put the boathook down twenty times. All over the place. Half of the probes hit ash and charcoal on the bottom. The pit's at least twice as big as the ground floor of this house."

"And you dug on the side nearest the road and found handfuls of crumbled baked clay and half a pot, which you've drawn for me here but will not bring out of the cave to show me?"

"You know Snowy won't let me."

"I know. But I'd like to see some of the stuff you find." Finney's voice was wistful. "Tell it as it happened."

I closed my eyes so that I could remember everything in order.

The first thing Snowy and I had discovered that afternoon was a graying and then blackening of the sand in our shovels. The white road had continued just as before, but next to it we gradually uncovered the beginnings of a fire pit. We gave over the next hour or so to staking out its borders. It was four feet deep under the sand in some parts, filled with hard, blackened charcoal that went powdery in our hands. Then we found the half-pot and next to that, where the clay rose in a small hill, the beginnings of a low wall.

"Work shift changes," Snowy had said then. "You shovel, I'll carry. This is where we can't afford to dump sand on what we might want to dig later." And so we began the shoulder-breaking work of carrying our sand away. The bucket handles cut into Snowy's palms under the weight of the sand. After three stumbling trips down to the river he made a kind of yoke piece across his shoulders out of the boathook, carrying two buckets at a time that way. I dug the best I could with my splinted finger jolting me every time I touched the shovel against it, but it was better than carrying buckets.

After a little, Snowy joined me on his knees, for

there was no hard digging here. I'd put down the shovel, gone to the trowel, and then, with just my fingers, removed, spoonful at a time, the sand that filled a small room, about twenty inches square. How long had it been there? Who had built it? There were no answers. No answers at all.

The roof had caved in under the sand. Carefully we removed the tiny curved tiles, setting them down beside us in a pile. After the sand was cleared, parts of the walls fell in toward the middle. But the room itself was intact, almost undisturbed, as if it had been abandoned very suddenly. And around the outsides of the walls were ten more strange splash-pattern holes in the clay soil.

"In the room?" Finney prompted me.

"Inside the room were parts of hundreds of more pots. There was a sort of tablelike board along one wall, and a wheel."

"A wheel."

"A potter's wheel, Mr. Finney. Something like the one they have in the art room. Of course, it was only two and a half inches high," I added.

"Barney," Dr. Dorothy said from the kitchen doorway, "I want you to tell me what you think you have found down in the cave."

"I don't know," I said. "I don't have any idea."

"Somebody should go down and have a look," she said. "Somebody from Harvard. Somebody from—"

"No!" I said. "That's out of the question."

"But this may be a very important—"

Finney cut her off. "Dorothy, I have a pretty good idea of what the boys have found. It's a curiosity. I think what the boys have found is fifteen years old. Maybe thirty. Maybe five."

"What?" I asked.

"Well, we are dealing with a scale model road, statues, potter's wheel, and so forth," said Finney. "Nobody would have had the knowledge to make this village you're digging up before the sixties or seventies—or the fifties at the earliest. Proper excavations on Pompeii didn't even begin until the 1950s. Very little was published before then. Only a serious archaeologist would have had the knowledge to recreate something like this. Who could have known about the root holes? What you've found, boys, is a magnificent joke. Probably constructed by a hermit or maybe an escaped madman hiding out with nothing else to do. It's marvelous. But I'd bet my four-hundred-dollar handmade leg here that it's modern."

"Supposing," I said, "that it's a hundred thousand years old."

"Pennimen," said Finney, "there has never been any evidence of any human life in North America before the ancestors of the Indians, who date back at the very most to fifty thousand years ago. No human bones or sites have been discovered that are any earlier than that. Human life started in Africa, not here on this continent."

"Mr. Finney, when Snowy and I first went down, there were no footprints in the crust of the sand. No one had been there before us. Besides, how can you say human life started only where they happen to have found bones so far? There may be zillions of buried bones in all kinds of places. Just because they haven't been discovered yet doesn't mean anything. There might have been people here before the Indians' ancestors migrated over. They just haven't been found up to now." My voice had gotten quite hot.

"It's ten degrees out, Barney," chirped Dr. Dorothy. "And it's late. I will drive you back to campus. If you walk, that metal thing on your finger will freeze and give you frostbite."

In the car she was silent, like a great padded moose behind the wheel. Then all of a sudden she said, "Barney." I waited while she spun out of a small skid without any alarm at all. "Please turn out the cuffs of your pants for me, Barney." I placed one foot on the dashboard and turned the cuff inside out. "That's it. That's it," she said. In the cold blue moonlight her fingers reached for something, snapped it up, and with a smile at the road ahead she pocketed it.

"Thank you, Barney," said Dr. Dorothy like a robin.

In my room five minutes later I turned out the other cuff. In it were six or seven pieces of charred wood from the fire pit.

CHAPTER THIRTEEN

Silks slit open his mail while I recited "If." "What school have you decided on?" he asked me.

"Winchester, Mr. Silks. I've decided to stay on."

Silks's flush started at the jaw and worked its way up. He kept his voice low. "I will speak to your father myself," he said.

"He isn't home, Mr. Silks. He's on the road."

"Where on the road?" Silks asked, as if I'd said in jail. His letter opener was a tiny Excalibur, its home slot in a heavy lump of Lucite made to look something like an iceberg. He twiddled it in and out of the slot, trying it different ways.

"I'm not sure," I said. "He said he may call me tonight."

"Tell him to call me in the morning."

"It won't do any good, Mr. Silks. I've decided that

I want to stay. Mr. Silks, I will not make any trouble for you."

"You *are* trouble, boy," said Silks.

"I will not make any trouble for you," I repeated.

"Just what kind of trouble are you talking about?"

"Any kind. I will not open my mouth about anything I see or know."

Silks slicked his tongue over his front teeth. "Something may happen to you, Pennimen. I have no control over that. I can't throw boys out of school because they might do something."

And if they do, that would lose you your job, wouldn't it? I thought. *One more incident will do it.* "I will be very careful, Mr. Silks. I will keep out of everyone's way. Please let me finish out my year here." Sweat sprang into my armpits and trickled down the soft hairs on my spine. "I'm ready for my history and math exams," I added cheerfully.

Silks ignored this. "You will not go to Hotchkiss, Pennimen, or any other decent school in the country. I will see that you wind up in a military academy where they take bad boys like you and straighten them out. You might as well apply to Concord Military right now.

"I hope you're good at drill, Pennimen. And push-ups and getting up at four forty-five in the morning.

I hope you like uniforms." Here he pointed the silver tip of the sword at me just so. "The cadets drill hours a day, Pennimen. Study halls are supervised. Every waking minute is supervised. Room inspections are daily. If you can't bounce a silver dollar shoulder-high off your bed every morning, the commandant rips the whole bed to pieces and you remake it till it's tight as a drum. You get a foot locker, and if that isn't neat, you do Saturday drill. Marching around in a circle for three hours in the hot sun or the freezing sleet. You open your mouth to a senior classman and he'll put his knuckles in it. The uniform collars are high and tight, Pennimen. Wool. Thick, hard gray wool. They itch. You scratch your neck and you get latrine duty for a month. I know. I went to Virginia Military Academy and I'm proud of it. It made a man of me."

"Mr. Silks, I am going to stay."

Silks looked at me, and I caught his eyes dead on, which he didn't like. He cleaned an ear with a pinkie finger and studied it. "It might do you some good, after all," he said with a smile. "Yes, when your father calls, I will tell him I am recommending you for Concord Military Institute, where you can be a little cadet for four years. I will do that for you, Pennimen."

"May I have my exams now, Mr. Silks?"

"Take care of that finger, Pennimen."

At two thirty I took Finney's first key from the chain on my belt. No one was near the music room. No one in the hall. The door was partially hidden by a plywood and canvas set from last year's senior play. The key worked, and I slipped in and down a stairway, soundlessly closing and locking the door behind me.

For a few moments I nearly forgot about the cave. I flashed my light on the walls of the old kitchen. In front of me was a stove with twelve gas burners and four ovens. It was made of white enamel with blue flecks. I touched the surface—dust lay there, and grease. I figured the stove was big enough to cook a hundred meals, which of course it must have done every night for years. A couple of ten-gallon iron kettles still sat on the sink's wooden drainboard. On the wall above the kettles hung a girlie calendar from December 1951.

I let my light play on the calendar. Christmas vacation had been crossed out. This room had stopped existing sometime in that month of that year, I thought idly. Probably closed after Christmas break. One day the whole kitchen was canceled and it doesn't exist anymore. My thoughts dwindled away.

The old kitchen was caught in time, just like the cave, just like a dead fly in a long-retired spider web. I had stumbled into a piece of time from long before I'd been born. I didn't think I belonged in 1951. Did I really belong in the cave?

Snowy would be waiting for me in the stable. I shuffled through the room, my light glancing off dozens of glass-fronted cabinets, one with a dried wasps' nest the size of a basketball in it. The pantry lay beyond. There were cardboard cartons under the counters. My feet crunched some Styrofoam packing material. I kicked it out of my way. I found the passageway, a bricked tunnel with a curved roof that led on for a quarter of a mile. Then, abruptly, the tunnel stopped. At the head of the stairway that ended the corridor little peeps of light shot through the second door.

The keyhole was gummed up with rust and dirt. I had to rout it clean with my pocketknife, but at last that lock turned too, and when I barged out into the light, I found myself, as Finney had promised, between two unused cold frames, their glass all splintered and broken, on the far side of the stable.

Snowy was covered with mud.

"Snowy, have you been in the cave already?"

"Sixth grade had a class trip today," he answered.

"Our exams finished yesterday. I didn't go. I told them I'd lost my glasses. Nobody wants a blind boy on a trip to the art museum."

"Have you been in the cave?"

"I filled the splash holes, the ones Finney says are root holes, with plaster of paris. They should be dry by now."

We marched through crusty snow. I stumbled on, following Snowy's string and wondering if he ever changed the route we took. The same pine boughs seemed to brush my face and the same nettles to catch at my pants. In the beginning I hated walking blindfolded, as I was afraid I'd trip or run smack into a branch at forehead level, but now I felt more like a horse trudging a familiar track with Snowy as my rider. "Find anything new this morning?" I asked, trying to be conversational.

"Yeah."

"Well, thanks for letting me know," I answered him. "You want to tell me what it is?"

"It's better if you see for yourself."

Snowy's attitude and Snowy's routine never changed. My blindfold didn't come off until three complete turns in the entrance cavern after the tunnel crawl. Then, as we walked one slow foot in front of the other along the ledge, he turned the light on and I was permitted to see.

It would do no good, I knew, to hurry Snowy up. I knelt in the sand while he dug up one plaster-of-paris root mold. I took the other. There was nothing much interesting about them. When we'd cleaned the dark clay away from the sides, they just looked like ordinary white roots.

"How would you like to spend six months in the library trying to find out what kind of a root this is?" I asked Snowy.

He blinked. "What are you getting at?"

"Finney," I said. "If it weren't for him, we wouldn't even have known what the holes were. He'll find out what kind they are too. Aren't you glad we're letting the Finneys help us a little, Snowy?"

He didn't answer that. He just knelt in his mud-covered jeans and parka, looking off at the partly fallen-in little house we'd discovered the day before. "Barney, I found something made of gold."

"What? Where?"

"Promise you won't touch it," he said without explaining. I noticed then that he had tossed his sweater over something at the back wall of our dug-out potter's house when he was in the cave earlier that morning. There was a new pile of sand beyond it. We hadn't dug there before. Snowy waddled over to it on his knees and removed the sweater carefully.

"What do you think?" he said.

In the lantern's smoky light, at the fire pit's edge, was a humped disk of gold about the size of a fifty-cent piece. On it was embossed a man's face, with wild curly hair and closed eyes. Fencing the disk all around were a dozen delicate ivory spears, tapered and sharply pointed, curving inward. They were set in pairs. My hand reached toward the middle and was slapped away sharply by Snowy. "Don't touch!" he warned me.

"Why not?" I asked.

"What do you think those things are?" he asked me.

I brought the lantern a little closer. Once again I tried to touch one, and again Snowy slapped me back.

"Hey!" I said.

"Barney, be careful."

"Of what? These things are just swords or sabers," I said. "Sort of. What are you scared of?"

"You know what I think they are?"

"What?"

"Get your hands back, Barney. I think it's a trap."

"What kind of trap?" I said. "A mousetrap?"

"Don't laugh. Look carefully. In the middle is what looks like gold, right?"

"Right."

"Okay. If you put your hand in there, you're going to graze it against the tips of those spears. No way not. The face on the gold disk, the disk itself, has closed eyes. I think these are graves, Barney. I think when a man died, he was buried with a kind of death mask made of gold."

"So let's take a shovel and dig up the whole thing."

"Barney, did you know the Egyptians put lethal gas in some of their burial chambers to ward off tomb robbers? Are you crazy? Supposing there's a lump of plutonium under there? We could have a melt-down!"

I sighed. "Poisoned in the Pyramids" again. There was no arguing with Snowy. If he didn't think of plutonium, it would be Stone Age AIDS germs. I took a piece of rice paper from my supply, and against the sole of my boot I cut a crude circle, small enough to wedge onto the gold disk. With neither of us touching the ivory daggers, Snowy held the edges of the paper down with my pocketknife while I traced the design of the face, carefully slanting the pencil through the openings in between the spears. Then I did another picture of the whole ring as it sat in the sand, a side view.

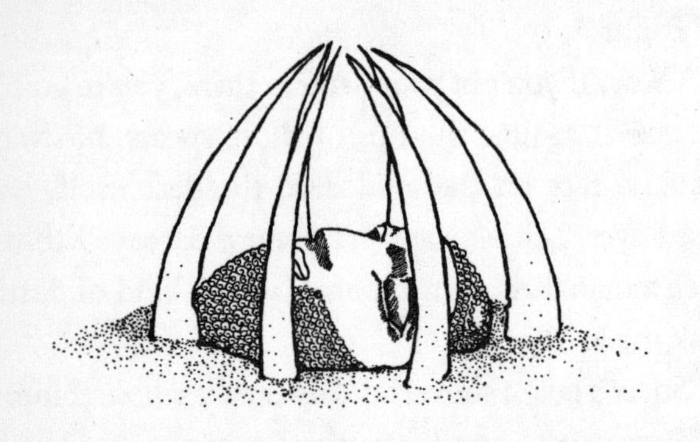

"There are more," said Snowy when I had finished.

"More what?"

"There are three more of these things. They're all on the rim of the fire pit. Look." He turned and gently brushed some sand from a small mound behind him. Another gold disk. Another face with eyes closed. Another ring of ivory spears. In the same snail-like procedure I traced the disk of this one and the one that lay beyond it, careful not to touch the surrounding spears, although I thought Snowy was crazy.

"I'm waiting for you to go into one of your King Tut stories," I said. "About how we'll both die horrible deaths for disturbing a tomb."

"You wouldn't listen," said Snowy distantly. "But you know what, Barney? Forget King Tut. You know how natives fight jungle warfare? You know what a punji stake is?"

"No, what's a punji stake?"

"They take some kind of very hard wood, okay? Like teak. And they carve it into spikes like knives. Then they soak the spikes in curare for a week. After that they plant 'em in the ground. Hidden under piled-up brush. You step on 'em and good-bye, Charlie. You're dead in twelve minutes. Central nervous system's paralyzed. You suffocate."

"Snowy, you believe everything you read," I said. I tapped one of the spears with my pencil. "Ivory, Snowy. Ivory can't soak up anything. My dad bought a pair of elephant tusks that used to sit right in the doorway of some Indian raja's bedroom. They're decoration. That's all."

There was a fluttering on the ceiling. The bats were making ready to go out. Ignoring Snowy's warnings, I reached down to retrieve my last tracing from the third gold disk. The little finger of my left hand brushed against the tip of one of the ivory spears. "Harmless!" I said to Snowy. "See?" My laughter echoed hollow, like the laughter of a ghost, throughout the cave.

CHAPTER FOURTEEN)

Four and a half weeks later, when the early March wind chased a clutch of winter clouds around the sky, I opened one eye.

I was alone. The window was open. I had no idea where or who I was. I lay there without moving because moving didn't seem to be a thing I could do. I only looked with that one eye and only out the window at the scudding clouds. A woman came into the room. *That's a nurse,* I heard a slow voice in my head say. *That's a nurse in a white uniform.* When she saw my open eye, she ran out of the room. More time passed, and then there were three men and another woman wearing a stethoscope hovering around me. Now I knew I was in a bed. I was in a hospital somewhere. I had no memory of anything bad or good.

"Can you hear me, Barney?" asked one of the

doctors slowly and distinctly, as if I were a six-month-old baboon.

"Of course," I said.

"He'll be all right. Get his father" was the next thing the doctor said. I closed my eye. I slept for two days.

When I woke, my father was sitting on my bed. We did not talk. He spoon-fed me custard pudding. I fell asleep again.

I woke sometime later with both eyes open. Another March day. Snowing this time. Someone was in the room, sitting on another bed. "Dad!" I said.

"You're awake!" he whispered.

"I'm awake."

"It's been a long time. It's been touch and go."

"It has?"

"Barney, it's March third. I've been here a month. Sleeping in this room. Only leaving you when Snowy or Mr. Finney or Dr. Dorothy spells me. You have been very sick."

"What happened? What happened to my hand? Why is it bandaged up like a watermelon?"

On the wall of my room I could see get-well cards. They were from the boys in my class.

"Do you remember anything?"

"No."

"You were in the cave."

"Yes. We were in the cave. Snowy and I."

Dad heaved himself off the bed. He put on a pair of glasses. I didn't remember that he wore glasses. Yes. He got them last year, of course. He lifted each of my eyelids and looked at my eyes. Then he felt my forehead. "Do you need the nurse?" he asked.

"No."

"Don't talk too much," Dad advised me. Sitting on my bed again, he began. "You know you must promise not to go back to the cave."

"Why?"

"Barney, you almost died. You were bitten by a snake."

"What? There wasn't any snake!"

"Barney, you just don't remember."

"I don't understand," I said.

"You keeled over after Snowy had walked you about halfway home. He got you to the school somehow. Carried you or dragged you. Five minutes into the emergency ward you went into cardiac arrest."

"I had a heart attack? I'm just a kid!" I said.

"Cardiac arrest can occur after a bad snakebite," said my father. "You swelled up like a balloon. Your little finger went iridescent red, bubbled up, and then started to go black. Everyone asked Snowy what happened. Snowy told the doctors his best guess was you had pricked yourself on a curare-filled punji stake. Well, you can imagine what the doctors thought of that. I flew here fifteen hours later. As soon as they got in touch with me. The Finneys had asked Snowy what you'd gotten into, and he had told them a lot of fluff about curses on tombs. He's fixated on punji stakes. That night he was so overwrought he said he'd go back to the cave and bring one out so that they could test it. You were about to die, you see. Well, they weren't about to have two boys bitten by snakes, so they told him if he ever went near the cave again, they'd throttle him and hobble his legs with chains.

"Meantime they tried everything on you. Cotton-mouth moccasin antivenin, copperhead antivenin, even rattlesnake. Snowy told me that just before you two left the cave, you went to pick something up. A drawing, I think. It was dark, Barney. You couldn't see. The snake was probably hibernating, and you disturbed it. We couldn't even see the bite afterward because your finger looked like a Sicilian sausage. Would you like some tea? I've brought a thermos."

"Yes, please."

Dad had also brought two fine bone-china cups, probably Limoges, with gold rims. I recognized them from the Finneys' china cabinet. Some things were coming back to my mind. I sipped, saying nothing.

"Is that tea all right? Do you want sugar?"

I nodded.

"Barney, are you ready for this?"

"Ready for what?"

"They had to take off your finger. The antivenins didn't work."

"Take off! What finger?"

"Fortunately it's the little one. Fortunately it's your left hand."

"Am I going to be all right?" I asked.

"Perfectly all right. You've lost the end two joints of the finger, but other than that you'll be fine. There is only one explanation for it.

"About ten years ago a crazy fundamentalist church group stopped near here. A traveling religion show. Snakes were part of the come-on. All kinds of foreign snakes we don't have antivenins for. You see, you have to use the right antivenin for the right snake. You can't use pit-viper antiserum on a coral snake bite. It won't take. Anyway, they set up their tent in Greenfield for a while in the summertime. They did all kinds of things, healing crippled people and chanting and coiling the snakes around their necks. The snakes had their venom glands removed and were harmless apparently. The preacher didn't tell that to the congregations, of course. So, to make a long story short, one of these snakes may have escaped pregnant. She may have been glandless, but her fifty little babies weren't."

"You mean they're in the cave? Grown-up now?"

"Barney, you may never go near that cave again."

"Never," I said groggily. The tea was warm and syrupy. It was beginning to make me sleepy.

"It got in the papers, you know," my father said wearily. "And naturally Mr. Silks is angry at you. The local papers carried the story. 'Prepster from exclusive Winchester Boy's Academy near death from copperhead bite.' Well, several boys' parents called the school worrying, you see. Silks figured that since you had once eaten toadstools on purpose, you had done this on purpose as well, to show off. Never mind. I think Silks thinks you've been neutralized for the rest of the year. But you must understand one thing. It is not safe for you to go back to the cave."

"How about Snowy?" I asked suddenly.

"While you were in a coma, Snowy spent every spare minute of his time right here by your bed, just looking at your face like a puppy. In the last few days he hasn't been around. We made him promise not to go near the cave. I hope he hasn't. But he's not my son. You are. And you're all I've got, Barney."

I fell asleep.

The next week, while my father was out to dinner, I opened my eyes, and there was Silks himself, standing at the foot of my bed looking like a funeral director. He asked me how I felt. I said, "Fine." Immediately he said "Fine" to that. And shifting his weight from foot to foot, gruffly offered me a booklet. "You should read that, Pennimen," he instructed me. In order not to have to talk to him anymore, I began reading right then and there. He edged out of the room muttering about getting me my textbooks and assignments.

The pamphlet was called *Safety First!* Published by the Department of Agriculture in 1941. It began by telling me that snakes are our friends. We must never kill them. We must never go near them. We must report them if they look strange. We must not pick them up. We must not disturb their young. It showed photographs of a 1941 boy about to put his foot in a dark hole where a snake lurked. *"Don't do this!"* the pamphlet shouted. There were pictures of people doing unimaginably stupid things to and with snakes. *"Don't do this!"* said the pamphlet each time.

One picture had a couple of eight-year-olds prodding a dead snake with a marshmallow fork. "We must not even touch a dead snake because the venom sits there in the glands behind the teeth, still potent, for at least fifty years," so there! When Silks was safely gone, I flipped the booklet like a Frisbee into the corner and called him an awful name.

When my dad came back that night, he began gently testing my memory of things. I was not so tired anymore. The memory test began simply, but soon it became a talk about old times. I remembered everything in the catalogues, where we'd found our best treasures, where we'd traveled.

"Am I okay?" I asked him.

"I think so, Barney. You will be, anyway, when we get you out of here. I wish you'd spend the rest of the term home. I wish I could go home with you. But if I miss a meeting next month in Stockholm, we'll go broke for the year. I'll call every night. Meantime I've arranged that you live at the Finneys' house, not the dorm."

"That's okay, Dad. Dad?"

"Yup?"

"You've been here a month? With me in the hospital?"

"Of course!"

"Didn't you have a convention somewhere? A buying trip in Italy?"

"Spain again. I canceled. I'll go as soon as you're well. You think I was going to go racing around Toledo and Barcelona with you flat on your back in a coma?"

During spring break, at the end of March, the bandage was taken off my hand. Everyone stood around waiting to see how I would react. The hand looked like a white prune. "You're lucky it's the left hand, and you're lucky it's only one finger," said someone for the hundredth time. I was put into physical therapy. I would be allowed to go back to school when the break ended, on April 1. I had lost twenty-one pounds. Everything had come back to my mind except the snakebite itself. I was well, except for the finger, which hurt where there was no finger left.

My father had mothered me the whole time. When I was well enough, he took me out to dinner at local steak houses every night, loading me with chops, lobsters, baked potatoes, and chocolate cream pies.

One night he asked me, a little shiftily, what Snowy and I had been doing in the cave in the first place.

I answered him just as shiftily with a question: "Did the Finneys tell you anything?"

"No," he said. "They seem to be honoring some promise to Snowy Cobb, although I can't imagine why. But I know you. You're not the caving type. Not unless there's something in the cave beside stalactites. What have you found down there?"

"I can't tell either, Dad. I made the same promise to Snowy. It's Snowy's cave."

My father munched a piece of pork chop. "Like father like son," he said, washing it down with a swig of beer. "I'm a treasure hunter, and you are too. You've found something. Someday, tell me."

"It's a deal, Dad. Someday."

"Are you going to be able to resist going back to whatever it is that's down there?"

I placed my little finger joint on the table between us. The skin at the end of the stump was pursed like a pouting mouth. I hoped in time this would get less ugly. "The difference between me and Snowy is that Snowy is an idiot and I'm not. The thought of fifty baby coral snakes or pit vipers or whatever they are down there, hiding in the sand . . . wild horses couldn't drag me. Are you kidding?" I attacked my spareribs.

The night before Dad left, he took an envelope

out of his coat pocket and pushed it across the restaurant table to me. It was a letter of acceptance from a prep school in Geneva, Switzerland for the following year.

"But I don't want to go to school in Switzerland," I blurted out.

"Barney," he said so sadly, "do you want to go to a military academy here?"

"No!"

"Well, then."

I played with the plastic netting that covered the candle glass between us.

The next afternoon, in the school driveway, my dad hugged me before he left for the airport. "Now, you promise? No more caving?"

"Dad, do you think I'm crazy?"

"Yes," he said.

"Dad," I said, "I've been having nightmares about snakes and snake-worshipping preachers since I woke up in the hospital." I buried my face in his shirt front.

Dad stood with his arms around me for ten minutes, roughing up my hair with his hand. He cried quietly. Then he blew his nose, fixed his tie, and said, "The Swiss aren't that bad, Barney." He drove away, waving sadly.

It was Saturday. March was almost over. Sunday night the other boys would be coming back from spring break. A long day spread before me. I had missed nearly a month's work. I had three papers due. I headed for the library.

By noon I'd finished enough note cards on Lincoln's cabinet to get a fair paper out of it. I had to prepare sketches on Roman architecture and research the uses of uranium in industry.

In the science stacks I passed by the ancient Latin encyclopedia of natural history that Snowy and I had pored over with the little bone in hand. Lazily I fingered the gold-stamped spines. Then I picked out the *S* volume. *S* for *serpentes.*

There were pictures of puff adders, fer-de-lances, and pit vipers. My hands sweated at the sight of them, slithery and deadly, even on the pages of an old book.

For the heck of it I tried reading the Latin text on venom and snakebite cures. It was not as difficult as I'd thought. After all, I'd had two and a half years of Latin. I began to enjoy it. I learned that snakes were milked for their venom and that the venom was injected into horses. The horse-converted serum, which contained antibodies to the venom, was what they'd put in my IV drip. Snake venom was extremely expensive and had to be stored at zero degrees centigrade. *"Toxicum post mortem serpentis indefinite permanet."*

I stared at the brightly hand-colored inset of cobras. The leading figure was the *Naja naja,* king of snakes, supple, risen from its coil with its little tongue peeking out of the cold lips and its hood thrown up like the mantle of a ghoul.

Like the cape on the strange black glass god. A chill rippled over my skin. There was also a picture of a snake charmer with a flute.

On one page, the only one in color was a full-size picture of the cobra's fangs. The *Naja*'s were about an inch long, curved like a tiny tusk, needle sharp, and down the center of the tooth lay a dark pillowed venom sac. *"Dentibus nolite tangere,"* said the Latin inscription. Do not touch the teeth! *"Toxicum post mortem serpentis indefinite permanet."* I translated aloud: "The poison lasts indefi—"

There was a slight noise behind me. I jerked my head around. Standing there was Snowy Cobb, covered with mud and smiling. "Are you ready, Barney?" he asked.

CHAPTER FIFTEEN

Snowy had brought down half a dozen kerosene lamps. One by one he lit them for me. Each lamp showed a new turn in a street, new buildings, carefully brushed clean of their sand. Soon a whole town spread over the floor of the cave, like a Christmas village in the glimmering lights.

I knelt there, tightness in my throat, fighting tears. "All by yourself, Snowy?"

"All by myself," Snowy answered. "For you, Barney. I thought you were a goner for a while."

I let his words fill the cave around us. Then we dove in.

The street leading away from our first house, the potter's shed, twisted on, lined with more impressive and complete buildings.

There was a house that appeared to be a carpenter's shop, with metal tools, saws, hammers hanging from the walls. Tiny nails, the size of a quarter of a straight pin, lay strewn around. Beyond that was what seemed to be a fish store, for a painted sign hung above it on the outside, a perfect shape of a fish in red and blue, and inside were long wooden tables, knives, and clay bowls set into the tables.

"Plumbing," said Snowy.

"What?"

"Look. See that clay bowl? That's a sink. Look under. There's a pipe leading from that to a bigger pipe under the street. I've dug it up a little. The whole place has thick fired clay pipes running down every street and into every house. They had running water."

There was a miller's shop, we guessed from a grindstone and a grayish powdery kind of flour that still remained in a wooden storage bin the size of a coffee can behind the back wall.

Most of the buildings had simple picture signs outside. We could understand a few but not all. There was a boot maker, a weapons shop with spears and arrows pictured in black and gold. Beyond the shops began the houses.

Snowy had excavated four. They were not full of furniture. They were not fancy. Only simple wooden board tables or maybe beds stood near the walls, and a few overturned half-barrellike stools for chairs. A jar or two leaned in the corners. There was straw in tiny pieces on some of them. Our kerosene lamps burned, and shadows crossed and recrossed the walls and sand that lay piled outside, where Snowy had carefully banked it so it would not fall back.

"What happened with the roots?" I asked him suddenly. "The plaster of paris you poured in? Did you take the molds to Dr. Dorothy? Mr. Finney?"

Snowy shook his head. "What could I do?" he asked. "Everybody thought you were going to die, Barney. The Finneys didn't want to know beans about the cave. They think it's full of African tree vipers. They told me I could never come back."

"Where are the root molds?"

"Over there. Right near the farthest lamp. Near our stove."

I held one of the molds up to the light. Sure enough, it looked just like a root all right. White plaster, of course, but knotted and gnarled like an old tree. It was as small as the root of a rose. "You see those little cut marks?" said Snowy, pointing.

"No."

"I'll show you in daylight," he said.

"Well, what about them?" I turned the root form in my hand and squinted at it.

"You know Mr. Greeves?"

"Well, of course I know Mr. Greeves! Come on, Snowy, out with it."

"Okay," said Snowy, drawing up his shoulders. "I brought them in to Mr. Greeves."

"Why Greeves?"

"Because one day I was in the art room after class, trying to replace the plaster of paris that I borrowed. He was working on his bonsai collection that he keeps on the windowsill."

"Those little miniature trees?"

"They keep the trees small by docking the roots. That way the tree grows strong but never too big. Greeves was docking roots all over the desk. I brought these in to him. He said he only did Japanese pines. Never saw roots like this, but they were bonsai all right, or something like it. The next day he came back with a book for me. We went through it. These are bonsai'd apple, nut, and peach trees, Barney."

I waited, kneeling in the cold sand, for him to go on. Knowing what his thoughts were.

"Barney, this is no fake. This is no model. This was real. This thing is over a hundred thousand years old. It goes back to the Ice Age. There were cobras here, Barney. Or something very much like them. And people, half a foot tall."

"Snowy, how do you know that for absolute sure?"

"Because the bit of charcoal you sneaked to Dr. Dorothy came back from some lab in California, where she sent it. That's how."

"What? She didn't tell me about it."

"Of course not. She doesn't want you curious about the cave. She thinks you'll lose a leg next time. I found the letter in the desk. You sneaked the charcoal to her. You took something out of the cave and didn't tell me you'd given it to her," Snowy growled.

"I didn't *take* anything. It fell out of my pants cuff in the car. She picked it up. Talk about sneaking, you went through their desk."

"You're damn right I did. I found the letter from the university and other things."

"What other things?" I wanted to shake Snowy.

"Nothing," he said lightly, but skewering me with a guilty look.

I knew I wouldn't get much out of him. "What did the lab say?" I asked.

"That charcoal is a hundred thousand years old, give or take ten thousand years. The bone must be that old too, Barney."

"The fire pit might be that old," I argued very weakly. "It might have resulted from a natural fire. Maybe before the cave was formed. Anything. And the houses and all the stuff could still have been done by a hermit ten years ago. The bone still could have been a very old bone carved very recently. The snake fangs—they could be very ancient, but they could also be five years old."

Snowy picked up a trowel and a paintbrush and handed me another paintbrush. "There's a building near the last lantern there," he said. "Bigger than the rest."

As we scraped and flicked the sand from around three brown adobe walls, I said to Snowy, "Now we can't talk to the Finneys about it anymore. If they find out we came back to the cave, I think they'll have a joint heart attack."

"It was your idea to talk to the Finneys in the first place, Barney," said Snowy. "Did you bring your pencils and drawing paper?"

"Yes."

"Look at that."

We were scooping the sand out of the inside of what was the biggest house of all so far. As the sand fell away from the walls, we could see they were decorated with paintings, paintings of a dance or festival. The floor of this house was not packed dirt but tiled in a mosaic pattern, whorls, blue and white with a red one in the center. There were stone benches and in the middle of the room a marble thing that looked like a small goblet.

"Fountain," said Snowy. "See the little hole it has in the bottom?"

We found a dozen more root holes. We decided we'd hit a garden of some kind, as the roof was open and made a courtyard. The house continued for many rooms beyond.

That night, when we reached the stable, Snowy took my blindfold off and filled a bucket of water at the tap in the old tack room.

"What's up?" I asked.

"You'll see."

He showed me a new arrangement he had set up in a horribly dirty old bathroom at the back of the stable. He'd put a folding chair and a Coleman stove on the floor and rigged a makeshift burner over it by setting a barbecue grill on two cinder blocks. He lit the stove and put the bucket on the burner.

"Snowy, where do you get this stuff?" I asked. "Lanterns, stoves . . . "

"Out of a magazine," he answered. "Some of it I keep here. Some of it other places." When the water warmed, he gave me a cake of soap. We washed our hands carefully. He produced a bottle of Royal Navy intensive-care skin lotion, and I used that, following him. Then he washed his face, combed his hair, and brought out two complete sets of pants and shirts. We hung our muddy clothes on a rope to dry, and put on clean shoes. "They'll never know," he said smugly.

When I walked through the Finneys' door that night, Dr. Dorothy greeted me with a pat on the shoulder. "You look as if you've been in church," she said.

"Oh, I just spent the day in the library doing my papers," I answered.

But she peered at me with eyes that said *I'll bet you did.*

I spent the evening in the guest room upstairs, coloring in my painting of the garden courtyard we'd found that day. I tried thinking what the wall painting must have meant. It was a picture of a woman smiling, her eyes closed, in a strangely layered dress. In either hand she held a wriggling snake. Was this a religion? Was it some sort of death ceremony? The woman's smile made me think that whatever was depicted there was a symbolic ceremony and no one was about to be bitten, although I couldn't be sure what she was up to.

The Finneys usually went to bed by ten. I figured I was safe as I'd said I wanted to go to sleep. It was eleven before my painting was finished. At eleven ten there was a knock on the door.

"Dr. Dorothy!"

"I see you've got your paints out," she said. She chuckled. "I thought maybe you'd like some chocolate with whipped cream? It'll put more weight on you, and you'll sleep well. I'm sure you have a lot of work ahead of you at the library." In her hand was a Sheffield plate tray with two cups of cocoa, steaming away.

"I . . . well, thank you," I said, mumbling and shuffling backward toward my desk.

"May I come in, Barney?"

"Well, sure."

She sat on the bed, placing the tray on a chair. I shoved most of the drawings into a binder while she was doing this and scattered papers over the rest.

"Drawing again?" she asked, chirping in her always bubbly voice.

"I was just now doing sketches of Roman architecture for Latin class. I've got a month's work to make up."

"I am sure you'll do splendidly, Barney." She blew slightly on the surface of her cocoa. As usual Dr. Dorothy's hair spilled out of the bun that she piled it in with a dozen hairpins. As always her skirt and jacket were heathery tweed, the good heavy kind my dad buys when he's in London. She had taken off her lab apron. Under it was a silk blouse and a strand of pearls. Her glasses hung on a red ribbon over her massive bosom, and she gazed at me as if she could see right through to the cells of my brain. "Drink your cocoa, Barney. I must talk to you."

I swallowed a hot mouthful of it too fast. I felt the whipped cream stay on my upper lip. She handed me a napkin embroidered with forget-me-nots.

"Yes?" I said, my tongue still burning.

"I must ask you something without telling you much at all. I can't."

"Why?"

"Because I am not free to say anything. What I can tell you is that I know you went back to the cave. You must not do it again. You gave your word to your father, and your father placed you in our care for the rest of the school term. If Mr. Finney finds out you went back to the cave, the consequences will be very bad for you, Barney." She paused and straightened out the ribbon that held her glasses. "When a boy gives his word, Mr. Finney takes it very seriously."

"I . . . I know," I said, feeling myself go the color of a Delicious apple.

"You were there today, weren't you, Barney?"

"I . . . I was in the library today," I said, my voice sliding up and then cracking a little.

"You're too clean for the library, Barney. You have scrubbed yourself like an acolyte. That can mean only one thing."

"Dr. Dorothy, there are no snakes in that cave. There are snake fangs but no snakes," I blurted out.

"Snake fangs? What on earth are you talking about?"

She examined my drawings for a very long time, her cocoa cooling and forming a skin in the cup beside her.

"A cobra?" she said at last. "A cobra here in Massachusetts?"

"How can I put this?" I said. "The antivenins they used on me didn't work. There's a whole list of antivenins in an encyclopedia of natural history in the library. I looked it up. A cobra bite has to be treated with an antivenin they make up in India. They didn't use that one on me because they didn't think I could have been bitten by a cobra. Besides, the fangs in my drawings are exactly like the cobra fangs in the book. The snake's called a *Naja naja.* It has one of the most deadly venoms in the world. Those little prongs, I thought they were spears, ivory spears at first. They're cobra fangs."

"That's preposterous," said Dr. Dorothy. "Cobras live only in hot climates."

"But, Dr. Dorothy, first of all, do you know what the climate was like here in Massachusetts, say a hundred thousand years ago?"

"No, but—"

"Well, could a cobra or a snake like a cobra live in a temperate climate, something like we have now?"

"Possibly. But you're talking about cobras in freezing caves, Barney."

"That's exactly it."

"What's exactly it?"

"I believe the snakes lived here in the wild and were brought into the cave, where they died. A hundred thousand years ago. I don't know how long ago. But that's what I believe."

"By whom, may I ask? A race of people six inches tall? Cobras get to be six feet long, Barney."

"Dr. Dorothy, we spent months in sixth grade learning how the Egyptians made pyramids as big as New York City skyscrapers almost with their bare hands. Without any steam shovels or electricity or metal or anything. Amazing things have happened. How could trees have grown inside a cave without sunlight? We don't know, but they did. I don't know if the snakes were drugged or trapped or if they played the flute and danced for them, but somehow this happened too, thousands and thousands of years ago."

Dr. Dorothy sighed and glanced as if for God's help at the ceiling light in my room.

"But the venom. It couldn't possibly last that long."

"Dr. Dorothy," I said, "in the encyclopedia, even in a stupid pamphlet Mr. Silks gave me, it says venom has been tested and lasts on and on, indefinitely. Providing it's kept at a below-freezing temperature. They haven't tested it for long enough to know how long it does last. The cave is below freezing. The cave is the perfect temperature for storing venom, keeping it live. They store it in the medical labs at that temperature."

Dr. Dorothy just stared. She clicked the string of pearls she was wearing between her fingers. Finally she said, "This puts me in an awful spot."

"Why?"

"If you bring me one of the fangs you describe and I test it and the test is positive . . . " Her words stopped, and she stared again, at the light on my desk. "Mr. Finney will find this whole thing difficult to swallow," she went on at last. "If you go back to the cave, he may be so angry that—"

"Dr. Dorothy," I burst in, "I'll take that chance. If Mr. Finney is furious, I guess I'll have to live in the dorm again. He'll kick me out of the house. But you can see my drawings for yourself, Dr. Dorothy. Please show them to Mr. Finney. Please convince him." I put my head suddenly in my hands and just held it there like a heavy weight. "It's not as if I'm doing anything bad, you know. We've found something wonderful down there."

Dr. Dorothy picked invisible lint from the front of her blouse. "I am a scientist, Barney. I understand."

"Well, do I have your permission to keep digging, then?"

"I'd like to see one of the fangs for myself, Barney. Bring me one of the fangs. Take it out ever so carefully by digging around it with a long-handled shovel. I can test it myself in my lab by injecting a tiny bit of it into a rat. If the venom is still live, I will talk to Mr. Finney myself on your behalf."

"But Snowy won't let me take anything out of the cave. If I even suggested it to him, if he caught me, he'd never take me back again."

Dr. Dorothy sat straight-spined, her eyes skimming over my drawings. She inspected the cobra god and the tracings of the gold disks, and a drawing of a broken clay pot.

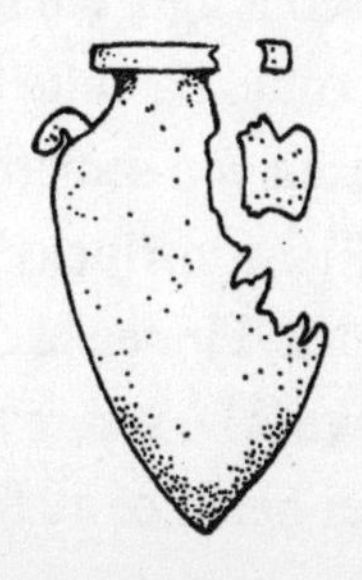

She went over my painting of the fresco we'd found on the wall that afternoon and my careful floor plans of each house. "Another thing I wasn't going to tell you, Barney." She stopped and looked at the skin that had formed on her cocoa and decided not to try it. "But since you insist on going back. . . . A couple of months ago I found a piece of charcoal in your pants cuff. I sent it off to a lab in Pasadena. Embedded in this charcoal were bits of molten glass, which were tested by a process called potassium argon dating."

"Oh? How old was it?"

"Somewhere in the neighborhood of a hundred thousand years."

"Does Mr. Finney know?"

"Of course he knows. He said it could easily have come from a forest fire during one of the ice ages. Ninety thousand years ago the cave may not have even been formed. People find charcoal from trees struck by lightning aeons ago. He still says the other things you've found could be quite modern."

"I wish I could bring you something," I said.

"Do this, Barney," she instructed, her eyes dreamy now. "We must get Mr. Finney back on our side. He may let you in the cave if he is sure there is no danger to you. Have you ever heard of a Havahart trap?"

"I don't like this idea one bit," said Snowy. Blindly I followed along through the woods behind him, string in one hand and cage in the other.

"It's a rat, Snowy, not a guinea pig."

"A rat has feelings."

"Snowy, the rat has been given enough morphine by Dr. Dorothy to let it go through a nuclear bomb blast without noticing anything."

"It's killing all the same," said Snowy.

"The rat has a brain tumor, Snowy. It's going to die anyway very soon. It's an old rat."

"You better do the whole thing."

"I told you I'd do the whole thing," I said wearily. I had assured him of that at least seven times.

Snowy huffed and fussed all the way to the cave. He set to work by himself, not saying a word to me, way down at the farthest point of our digging. I took the wooden box and set it gently in the sand. The rat was beginning to come to after its morphine, and I wanted to hurry and not let it escape. Very slowly I stuck a piece of bacon in the far end of the box, watched while the rat smelled it and then shuffled over to it. While it was eating at one end of the trap I pulled out the removable bottom slat on the other.

In one motion I slapped the whole box, rat inside, over one of the rings of cobra teeth. Then I dropped three pieces of bacon and two chunks of cheese right in the middle of the disk.

"Good-bye, rat," I said, and left it there. It would probably scratch itself and be dead in two minutes.

For the next hour Snowy and I excavated what we called the Rich Man's House, because of its garden and columns and paintings. There were eight rooms in this house. All empty and all decorated with miniature paintings of more fabulous jumping scenes involving weird-looking animals and smiling women. There was plumbing here all through the building. We found what seemed to be a pool, as the bottom was tiled and lined with a mosaic of fish. But what fish! Flying fish! Fish with legs, fish with horns on their heads. All no bigger than pictures on postage stamps. There were no signs of snakes in the paintings.

"Do you think the rat's dead yet?" Snowy asked, not looking at me.

"I'll see. Gee. It's been an hour and a half."

I wandered back to the rat cage and looked in the wire side. The rat was running around like a mechanical toy. It must have hit all the fangs by this time. The bacon and cheese were gone from the disk.

There was no way this plump rat could have slithered between the fangs and gotten at the food. It had to have climbed into the circle of deadly points. But it was alive still. Why?

Poor thing's probably cold, I said to myself. I opened the top hole of the cage and dropped more bacon and pieces of cheddar onto the disk, and this time left my lantern there to keep the rat warm.

"Still kicking," I said to Snowy. We dug for another length of time and uncovered two outbuildings near the main part of the Rich Man's House. Then I went back.

The rat lay dead in the back of the cage. Only one piece of bacon had been nibbled. The heat from the lantern had melted the cheddar cheese over the gold face on the disk. "Dead!" I yelled to Snowy.

"You pick up the body," said Snowy. "I don't want to see it."

"Don't worry!" I called back. I lifted the box carefully off the circle of fangs and poked the rat a couple of times to make sure he was dead. "Thanks, old man," I murmured to the rat. It was funny . . . the lantern had something to do with this. . . . But of course. I knelt in the sand. The venom must have been frozen solid until I left the light on top of the cage. Two months before there had been a lantern sitting there for half an hour while I'd traced the faces on the disks. Then I'd reached down in for my little tracing and cut my finger. . . . The heat had liquefied and activated the poison. How long would it have stayed frozen? Forever?

I could see Snowy's back turned to me in disgust as he dug about twenty yards away. This was my chance. Hardly moving, I took my trowel, dug up one of the fangs, and shoveled it carefully into the box with the rat.

That evening I presented Dr. Dorothy with the rat's body. While Snowy was doing dishes I brought out the tooth.

"You got one! Does he know?" she whispered, looking over at Snowy, who was fixing Rosie's bedding.

"No. Don't let him see it."

Dr. Dorothy took the fang into her lab and, using a series of needles and a suction tube, emptied it of venom. The venom was dark yellow. There were only two drops. Then she withdrew some blood from the rat and told me to go upstairs for an hour.

An hour turned into two hours. I had plenty of homework to fill the time. But I fidgeted over it, trying to overhear if she was talking with Finney yet or still doing tests in her lab.

I did not know until morning. Then, when she'd driven us up to school and Snowy had left the car and raced ahead to class, she slipped a small ring box to me. "The tooth's in there," she said. "The venom was live all right. You knew that when the rat died, though."

"Did you talk to Mr. Finney?" I asked. "Is he mad at me? Is he going to make me live in the dorm again?"

"You may stay with us, Barney," said Dr. Dorothy. "He doesn't want you back at the dorm with those boys. He promised your father he'd see you safely through the year."

"Is he angry?"

"Yes. Of course, I told him I sent you back myself. To get the tooth. He was furious at me for doing that, because I didn't really know for sure there were no live snakes down there. Mostly he was hurt that you just went galloping off with Snowy the day your father left. That you gave your word and broke it. You see, when your dad left you in our care, naturally Mr. Finney swore on a stack of Bibles you'd never set foot in the cave again. He gave his word. You broke yours, and that makes my husband look irresponsible."

I slumped against the car seat. Her hands rested

on the steering wheel, and she was staring straight out the windshield. The car heater hummed and coughed. "Mr. Finney is a difficult man sometimes," she said gently. "He had great faith in you, Barney. He told me after Christmas break, 'There's a boy who'll become a good man. He won't lie or sneak for the rest of his days. I know my boys. And he's a good one.' "

"And now he thinks I'm the same rotten kid he almost threw out?"

"I wouldn't go that far. Come on, you'll be late for class."

"Can I . . . is it all right with him if I go back in the cave now?"

"Yes, Barney. He knows it isn't dangerous. But for him it's a matter of honor. Mr. Finney is not much interested in what you find anymore. He is now convinced that this silly snake group, these religious nuts who passed through with their boa constrictors and probably cobras five or six years ago, planted the whole thing, carved up the statues and the whole village you've found and did a good job of it too. He said they were just the type."

"Do you think that too, Dr. Dorothy?"

"Barney," said Dr. Dorothy.

"Yes?"

"Let it stay your secret. Yours and Snowy's. As it began."

But there was another secret. Something Dr. Dorothy was not telling me. I'd heard it in her voice the night before and saw it in the eyes that looked through the windshield, not at me.

CHAPTER SIXTEEN)

"We are free, Snowy, free at last," I said to him at the beginning of that afternoon's trip. "Finney's let us back in the cave, even if he does think the whole thing's a fake, and we're in fat city."

The woods had changed in spring. Where heavy fir boughs had once tossed snow in my face, they only brushed my head softly. Where we had slipped and crunched over ice and snow, only a soft bed of mud and pine needles lay underfoot. I could smell the newness of the green leaves. "Even the boys are nice to me now," I said.

"Rudy? Danny?" Snowy asked with some amazement edging his voice.

"No. Not Rudy and Danny. The other boys in the class, though. They all love to see my finger. They can't get enough of it. They keep asking me how big the snake was. Was it under a rock? What happened?

Most of them want to go out and find themselves a cottonmouth now. I told them I touched a dead snake's tooth, that was all. Even Silks is quiet for a change. I don't have to recite every morning in his office anymore."

Mr. Silks, after inquiring about my finger silently by staring directly at the stump, had said only one thing to me since spring term had begun. He had been notified by my dad that I was to attend high school "out of the country," as he put it. I had nodded vaguely, wondering if he would sabotage Geneva too. Apparently he had no intention of doing this but only smiled frostily and victoriously. Fixing his silver letter opener securely in the slot of its Lucite blob, he told me that the Lycée de Notre Dame in Geneva was run by a bunch of friars. Chapel attendance was required every morning at seven, and the whole school was conducted entirely in French, which I'd better go learn in a hurry. On balance he thought it would do me even more good than a military academy.

"What about the five boys?" Snowy persisted.

"They look at me the way they always have. Mean as guard dogs in a gas station. But they can't do anything, Snowy. I disappear right after classes, and they can't touch me at the Finneys'. They know it too."

"If I were you," said Snowy, "I'd order a few cans of Mace."

"If we could fit it through the tunnel," I said, "I'd order a leaf blower."

"Why?"

"Snowy, we've got just these two months. Three weeks in April and then May. June fifth school is over. We don't have much time. At least I don't. You'll be back next year. If we had a leaf blower, we could blow the sand right off half the buildings down there in an hour. You're lucky, Snowy. You've got two more years here. You'll probably find a trove of diamonds or something while I'm chattering away to a bunch of French monks."

I could not see Snowy's face. He was tramping on ahead of me, and I was blindfolded. Was I becoming more sensitive to sounds and voices, not being able to see? It seemed to me he had sighed, was just on the point of saying something, and then decided against it.

"Snowy, what is it?"

"What do you mean?"

"Dr. Dorothy is keeping something from me. Do you know something I don't know?"

No answer.

"Snowy, for crying out loud! Say something."

"I don't want to."

"Why not?"

"No."

I stopped dead in my tracks. "You have to tell me," I said.

"I don't have to tell you anything. Come on. We don't have all day." He yanked at the string I held in my hands.

I wouldn't budge. "Snowy, I'm still here at Winchester, not just for the cave but because I wouldn't sleep nights thinking the gang was after you. You owe me one now. Tell me."

Snowy did not answer for quite a while. I could hear his boots scuffing the leaves underfoot. Finally he spoke. "Okay. Remember I said I sort of looked in their desk and all? Found the letter from the university saying the charcoal had been dated?"

"Go on."

"There was another letter."

"Who from? Come on, Snowy. Who from?"

"Exeter."

"Exeter!"

"Finney's been offered a job as dean of students. Not headmaster, dean of students. One rung underneath. Exeter's pretty hot stuff, though. Toughest school in the country."

Something began falling into place in my mind, like cards leaned end on end in a chain and pushed, falling one by one. Snowy had turned and had begun walking again. I followed him. "Did you read the whole of the letter?" I asked him.

"I glanced at it," he answered stiffly.

"What did it say?"

"Oh, the usual formal junk and stuff about salary and housing and all, and they also said . . . I don't exactly remember the wording. Something about we would be pleased to include the boy you recommended so highly, providing his final grades are . . . whatever."

"What?"

"I don't know. I guess Finney wanted to pull somebody into Exeter. It couldn't be me. I'm a sixth grader. Exeter starts in ninth grade."

"What do you mean, *wanted* to pull, Snowy?" But I knew.

"Well, I don't think he'll take you into Exeter now, Barney. We went back to the cave. We broke our word. You promised him and your dad. You know how Finney is about honor and all that stuff. I'm sorry. I didn't want to tell you about the letter. I thought it was better you didn't know anyway."

I kicked angrily at a log in our path. We had

reached the entrance of the cave. Lilac, sweet smelling as any living thing on earth, flowered somewhere. To me it might as well have been rotten eggs. I had wrecked my chances of going to the best school in America. My father would hit the ceiling when he found out.

I followed Snowy in silence to the entrance of the cave, choking back tears. Geneva loomed ahead. Four years of speaking nothing but French. Then what would happen? I could become a waiter. I'd rather go to cadet school. At least they might have hamburgers and potato chips once in a while.

Snowy turned and took my blindfold off at the entrance to the ledge. "You're, um, crying, Barney. I guess we blew it."

"I guess I blew it, Snowy," I said. I wiped my eyes on my sleeve. "I only know one thing in French."

"What's that?"

"Ça n'existe pas."

"What does that mean?"

"Basically it means, forget the whole thing."

That afternoon we found the temple.

It was quite by accident. If I could have pictured a city with a center, with rougher, poorer buildings on the outside and richer, more elaborate ones as you worked your way inward, I would have expected it to be higher in the center than at the edges. But there was no upward in the cave. We noticed, though, that one of the roads led down. It was made of stone, the same cut blocks as before, but then it widened and became a set of steps.

The steps themselves then fanned out, as though they were set in a large circle, like the steps in an amphitheater. On the third level of stairs, inset in the stone, was a tiny silver squiggle running downward like a streak of mercury. I cleared the next step down. The silver thread thickened and ran down the next riser and kept going. I followed it with my trowel and brush. The steps and silver inset became broader. I brought the lantern over. "Look, Snowy."

He lay at eye level with it. "Can't see a thing," he admitted. "Looks like a trail of metal in the stone."

"Okay. Trust my eyes. We have eight steps cleared here. This silver is a snake's tail leading down. See? It gets wider as it goes. I bet anything that at the bottom it turns into a full hooded cobra, all made of silver. As soon as it gets wide enough, there will be scales tooled into the metal. In a pattern. Just like the black god's cape."

I lay on my stomach and tapped at the widest bit of gleaming snake body we'd uncovered. "It's real silver, Snowy. I can tell. I can tell by the way it sounds and the way the metallic surface shines in the light."

Snowy put out a finger. Closing his eyes, he said, "I can feel the scales. Just."

"Do we dig out all the way around the whole circle of steps or dig straight down?" I asked Snowy.

"Down, I think. Let's see how deep it is."

"Snowy," I said, "I have a feeling. I can't explain—"

Snowy broke in, "As if the air . . . or something were different?"

"As if something were almost alive here!" I whispered.

Digging down could have been as frustrating as our original bout with the endless road. But the silver snake body grew broader and more beautifully carved, and we knew it would lead to somewhere soon.

We had to go on bucket shifts to remove the sand. I calculated the circumference of the circle, based on the curve of the steps we had exposed. It looked to be at least a hundred feet around, probably more. How deep? How many cubic yards of sand had to be removed? On one of my trips to the river with the buckets I thought about replacing the tooth, which sat ever in my pocket in its little box. I could slip it back in its ring around the disk without Snowy seeing me, but I broke into a new sweat considering it. If Snowy found I'd taken something out, he might get hideously, unreasonably angry. I might never see the finish of what we had started. The tooth stayed in my pants pocket. Snowy turned and called me. Not the time to go bending over the gold disks.

He had taken the boathook and jabbed it down in a spot toward the center of the circle. It sank all the way into the sand at his pushing. "The boathook's five feet long, and it still hasn't hit bottom," he grumbled impatiently. "We'll be digging these steps till kingdom come!"

Instead we decided to take one level of steps and follow it around its complete circle. This was only paintbrush work. The curve continued perfectly. Every few feet or so along there was a new part of the serpent's tail, identical to the last. "All the tails lead down the same way. It's a pattern. There must be forty of them. What could it be?" Snowy asked.

"What are these?" I asked. I pointed to a new marking that was carved into the stone risers, the vertical part of the steps, on the eighth level down, around the circle regular as a wallpaper design.

Because I couldn't sink myself into the sand to get below them and have a look, Snowy crept around the circle and felt with his fingertips. "Trace a few,

Barney," he said excitedly. "I think we've found . . . writing. Something like writing."

Leaning over and placing my paper on the small designs cut into the stone, I traced twenty of them while Snowy went on clearing steps. When I had finished, I had a row of strange figures.

"It makes no sense," I said, peering at it.

But Snowy stopped all work, spread my paper under a lantern, and stared at it, became lost in it, like an owl over a rabbit hole.

I took the boathook and, walking slowly, tracking it behind me, made a huge ring in the sand where I guessed the outer edge of the circle of steps lay. "It's this big probably," I announced to him, standing in the middle. "It must be forty feet across." I jabbed the boathook down. "We don't have time to . . . " I stopped. The boathook had hit something hard right in the middle of the circle. I poked again. Snowy heard it. He came running over with one of our big shovels. We dug at the hard surface until we had uncovered a little of it. Solid stone. White. Blank.

For a half an hour we made soundings with the boathook. We pushed it down as far as it would go, pulled it out, and tried to measure the depth of the sand in different places. The boathook hit stone only in the middle of the circle. We squared off that portion and began digging at the edges. What we discovered was an oblong roof. The little trench we dug along one edge showed columns, also made of stone, but delicately carved with vines and leaves twining around them. In the vines were tiny birds.

Under this, like a layered wedding cake, was another slightly larger platform, and under that more columns. These had different vines carved on them, fruit-bearing ones. "What we have, I think, Snowy, is the top of the biggest building yet. It's in the middle of a forty-foot circle of stone steps leading down. Its foundations are sitting in a deep pit. There's an awful lot of sand to clear away. Is it worth it or should we go on with the village?"

Snowy had cleared away more sand from the second layer of roof. He had exposed the side of a third platform and began freeing up a third set of columns. These columns were not twined with grape or rose vines. They were wrapped around with silver snakes. If my math held, the third-down story of the building would be about five feet by two and a half with a column every foot along each side. Fourteen tapered shafts of marble stood in that encrusted sand, each with a gleaming cobra, its pin-small forked tongue extended and its hood full out.

"What do you think, Snowy?" I asked, giving him a hand to his feet.

He'd dropped his glasses. He retrieved them, cleaned them on his shirttail, and said with his beady little eyes almost sightless, "Worth it, Barney? Are you kidding? It's worth more than everything so far put together. Do you know what this is?"

"No."

"This is the big find, Barney. The main event. I'm going to figure out the code you traced if it kills me."

Two buckets and two boys do not make sand move fast. After three days we had exposed the whole rim of the circle, which was about a hundred and twenty-five feet around, and cleared the sand for twenty steps down. We could see silver snakes, beautifully worked, embedded in the marble steps now, all leading down toward the center of the pit. The beginning of the next week we changed tack and began digging a two-and-a-half-foot-wide trench down the stairs, following a winding silver snake body to see how far the steps went down. The *S*-shaped back curved out of our digging range sometimes, but we always hit the next bit of it three or four steps down. The farther we went, the wider our trench had to be at the top, and as we got close to the center it was nearly twenty feet across at the surface. After a week of digging we hit bottom. There were eighty steps down, and the pit was ten feet deep in the center.

Dr. Dorothy caught me alone at breakfast the next morning while Snowy (and Rosie) were in the bathroom.

"Barney," she said, putting a healthy ounce of heavy cream into her coffee, "I have been looking at your drawings carefully. Why are there no stoves or fireplaces or ovens in any of the houses?"

"I don't know."

"Don't you think there would be if they had been used?"

"There's the huge fire pit."

"But why use that?" she asked. Her spoon made a marbled swirl of black coffee and white cream.

"I don't know. I never thought about it."

"I have. It's not such a mystery, Barney. Have you ever seen the model villages they have in natural history museums? Everything from Eskimos to Zulus to Babylonians? All with everything exactly in scale?"

"Yes, I have. On last year's class trip to New York we went to the Museum of Natural History. The year before to the Museum of Science in Boston."

"Did you notice that all the models have some cooking or heating or even clay-firing facility?"

"Yes. Yes, I think so. They make it look real with red glass for embers, and they put a tiny red spotlight in the corner of the case, beamed right at it to make it glow like real fire."

"Yes," said Dr. Dorothy. "But there are no primitive stoves or ovens in the models you've found. There are fired clay pots but no kilns to fire them in."

"They must have been fired in the fire pit," I repeated.

"It's funny," she said. "If it were a scale model, even a very, very old one, surely the model maker would have included provisions for fire, life's great necessity, along with all the other carefully carved objects. There's only one reason I can think of that he didn't."

"What's that?"

Dr. Dorothy brushed some crumbs into her napkin. "Because," she said, "fire is fire, and it is the size it is no matter what. It is the only thing you cannot have in small quantities. It cannot be miniaturized. A fire to scale in one of your buildings would burn out and be useless in two minutes. Therefore a very large fire pit, just as you have found, would have to be used for heat, baking, and so forth."

"Yes?" I answered.

"Well, it seems to me that if Mr. Finney is right and all you have found down there is the work of a clever hermit, or a bunch of snake worshipping cranks, they would have to have been very clever indeed *not* to put in little hearths and chimneys and cooking facilities. That's too clever."

"Do you mean," I asked, "that you think it was actually used, lived in? That there was a race of six-inch-tall people during the Pliocene?"

"I have said what I've said," said Dr. Dorothy, clearing her place. "And that is all. I'm a scientist, Barney. I can't tell you any more without proof."

Snowy came jouncing down the stairs, Rosie in hand. "That's all," Dr. Dorothy whispered and added in a louder voice, "Have a good day in school, boys. Don't break any rules!"

CHAPTER SEVENTEEN)

Snowy put Rosie in her laundry basket. He had retired the grapefruit crate. It was too confining. Rosie was a very pregnant guinea pig. He had made her a soft bed of velveteen strips from an old pillow. She sat in there snuffling her pink nose and closing her eyes, which were small and beady, just like Snowy's.

Hours of sand bailing lay ahead again that afternoon. I had calculated the volume of the buckets, the volume of the sand we had to clean, and the time it took us to dig, carry, and dump each pailful. It was now April 18. If we could work every single schoolday from two thirty to dinnertime, and every weekend day, we might get it cleared by the third week in May. That would give me a good three or four hours to study at night so I would be ready for review week before final exams.

Mondays through Fridays we cleared the sand from around the building, which grew cheeringly larger and larger. Weekends we worked on the circle of steps. So far there were only bodies of snakes, no heads. The cobra hoods and heads were still beneath the surface. The bottom level of the building would have to be about ten by five feet, I figured, given the progressively larger stories on each level. We had by now uncovered most of six floors. The columns wound with snakes continued down for another level, to the fourth level from the top. Then the walls were solid but with windows every foot or so. The windows were in the shape of drops of water or pears, we couldn't tell which.

During school hours I kept to myself. I did not show the boys in school my chopped-off finger anymore. I did not want anyone to ask why I had calluses like a dirt farmer on my hands.

The week before finals classes would be given over to review. Afternoons and evenings would be spent cramming. If I did not cram, I would not get above a B average. No one could, except for Snowy, who seemed to know the work that he liked by heart and settled for a C plus for the rest. On my last day for two weeks in the cave, I dug like a starving dog in search of a marrowbone.

If you can picture a round swimming pool, about ten feet deep and forty feet across, the bottom covered with sand, stairs sloping down the sides, as in a stadium, and in the middle a building like a wedding cake, that is what we faced. The floor was still hidden from view by the sand, and on the floor was what we sought, I knew. Whether it was proof of the age of this whole civilization we'd discovered or an explanation of what it was about, I didn't know, but I knew it lay there because this was the center of everything in our secret small world of the cave.

By six thirty on the Sunday evening before review week, we'd cleared a little of the floor, enough at least to reveal the hood and eyes and mouth of one of the silver cobras that adorned the steps. What lay around it and under the rest of the sand would be Snowy's to find. I would have to be content with seeing it after he'd uncovered it.

I had to be able to write three intelligent paragraphs on the motives of any of the main characters in *The Merchant of Venice* and *David Copperfield.* I had to be prepared to explain the conversion by chlorophyll of sunlight to energy in leaves, to translate any three pages of Caesar's *Gallic Wars* from the Latin, to deal with any of a year's worth of geometry problems, and to give a fair account of what went on in the administrations of Roosevelt, Taft, Wilson, Harding, Coolidge, and Hoover.

No one whispered to me in the library. No one asked me for my notes. At night when Snowy came back to the Finneys' from the cave, I begged him to tell me what he'd found, but all he ever would say was "You'll see when exams are over."

Finals were proctored by Silks himself, marching up and down the aisles of the class like a sentry, distracting everyone, throwing everyone into a cold sweat at the clomping approach of his tasseled loafers.

I did well. I don't know why I tried so hard. I guess because, in spite of the temple and all we had discovered, I kicked myself at night and lay in bed gnawing at my knuckles because I'd blown my chances of going to Exeter and my dad would one way or another find out. During the past six weeks Finney had been "away on business" most of the time. What that business was I knew well. He was getting himself settled at Exeter. But Dr. Dorothy never mentioned where he went, and there was no forgiveness for me. I guessed I deserved a bunch of French friars.

And so, on exams I did well the way a machine does well. I could not have cared less if chlorophyll converted sunlight into energy in toothpaste instead of leaves, if Portia had run for vice-president of the United States, of if the sum of the sides of a parallelogram was equal to a pint of maple-walnut ice cream.

Before we were allowed to leave each exam, Silks nearly stripped every boy to his underwear, examining shoes, feet, hand backs, palms, sleeves, and even hair before we were allowed to go. I knew he'd do something like this. I hadn't even dared bring my blank drawing paper and pencils with me.

At the last exam Silks called our names in alphabetical order. Fifty-three boys marched one by one to the desk. In a die-straight stack they piled their blue books next to Silks's personal Bible. Once in the hallway they let out a combination of noises very like an invasion of a kangaroo pen by whooping cranes.

I drifted through them, quietly making my way toward the music room, feeling my keys in my pocket. The night before, Snowy had relented and told me what he'd found while I'd been cramming. He'd figured out that we'd found an arena. He was taking first year Latin and had learned all about Roman gladiators, and something like a Roman gladiator arena was what we had found. But these gladiators had not fought with lions. They had fought with snakes.

The silver cobra heads had all met in a circle on the floor of the stadium, their hoods evenly embedded in the stone at the base of the temple. The stairs had ended at a foot-high circular wall, which was removed by a small empty moat from the inner floor. All around the sides of the wall, he told me, were scenes of men fighting coiled and ready-to-strike cobras. There were men dying and men plunging spears into the snakes' mouths. Women playing pipes at snakes. Men riding snakes and women holding snakes' heads high in victory. He could not wait until I drew it, he admitted. But that was not all.

Ringing the base of the temple were aboveground crypts. On each was another gold disk and the double fangs of the killer cobra set into the marble at the head. "Tombs, Barney," he'd said, his eyes all afire and his hands gently soothing Rosie. "Tombs with lids. We don't have to dig them up. We can pry a lid and look inside without disturbing them. I haven't done it yet. I've saved it for you!"

I'd wanted to hug him, but of course I didn't. Instead, I high-and-low-fived him, as if he'd hit a grand slam in the World Series, met his sparkling eyes with mine, and gave him three Tobler bars without nuts.

The lock to the old kitchen turned easily. I slipped in back of the play set and closed the door behind me.

I'd saved a giant-sized Tobler bar and bit out a big chunk as I went down the stairs in total darkness. Then I realized I'd left my drawing paper and pencils in my locker. "Dummy," I whispered aloud. Snowy would be waiting for me impatiently in the stable. I had to waste ten minutes running all the way to the classroom basement three buildings away where the lockers were.

When I came back, I did my usual check that no one was in the hall near the music room. Then I opened the old kitchen door again. I'd forgotten to relock it, and it pushed in with a click from the hinges no louder than a single sound from a cricket.

I stopped at the foot of the stairs and listened as I always did. There was no sound but the pummeling feet of newly released boys in the school above me. Satisfied, I ran my flashlight around the old kitchen, over the grease-encrusted stove, the sinks, the pantry beyond. I flicked it off. I stepped into the kitchen in the pitch dark and stopped. There was something wrong. I could see and hear nothing. But as my light had scanned the calendar above the drainboard for a moment I'd noticed the page had been changed to the month of June.

Whatever instinct I had forced me down into a squatting position and three silent steps backward.

There I waited like a catcher until I thought my knees would give out. Nothing happened. *All right,* my brain said logically. *Someone has been here, but that doesn't mean they are here now. Maybe it was just a caretaker.* I breathed like a mouse. *No one knows the kitchen like I do,* I told myself several times, slowly. I began edging forward toward the pantry. If anyone was here, they would be hiding along the walls. My opening the door would have given them fair warning to hide. I didn't dare go back up the stairs because they creaked a little. Had someone seen me go into the cellar? *No,* answered a logical voice. *But someone saw you come out and go back to your locker. You were not careful. You didn't look around. You didn't lock the door again. Someone saw you come out. They went down here to see where you were going. Now you've surprised them. They're hiding. Hiding someplace.*

In a straight line, on my hands and knees, I inched ahead. All my muscles and every cell in my brain focused on my hearing. I heard nothing. Then the sound of cloth, just cloth wrinkling against a shoulder or a leg. Where? Was it my own shirt I heard?

There were a hundred places in the old kitchen for someone to conceal himself. If I wanted, I could crouch unseen myself, soundlessly, behind a cabinet or under a sink—if I was lucky—but then I would be cornered like a rabbit in a hole. If somebody was in here, what were they waiting for?

I began trying to make myself see in the dark. Listening was seeing in the dark. My skin took on a way of listening. There were hairs on my forehead and the knuckles of my fingers that I hadn't known existed. I could feel if I was close to a wall or an object because the sense of solidness instead of open air warned every hair on my body whether I was near something or not.

The distance from the kitchen to the beginning of the long passageway was normally a ten-second stroll. I made it, counting seconds to steady myself, in eleven minutes. If they were here, why didn't they pounce on me? If they were here, why didn't they turn on a light? *Because,* said the god of logic, who was close by my ear, *the electricity is turned off down here, and they don't have flashlights.* I knew just where I was. Beside a row of water casks that sat on the pantry floor. To my left was another sink. Then I remembered the crunchy Styrofoam packing bubbles. I was careful not to step on them. It took me another six minutes to stash my own flashlight behind the casks. Then I padded on. Out toward the long brick passageway, out toward the door at the end. A distance of a hundred and fifty yards. I began to walk. If they were anywhere, they would not be here. They would not yet know where I was. They were blind and I was blind, but I was not as blind as they because every bit of me but my eyes was seeing, and I knew the territory. As quietly as a bird gliding I went farther and farther toward the exit. "*In the country of the blind,*" ran Mr. Greeves's words in my mind, "*the one-eyed man is king.*" *I am the one-eyed man,* I added to it. I reached the stairs at the far end of the tunnel. Now at least there were two minutes between me and the kitchen. I tiptoed the last set of steps, my legs aching in the effort not to make them creak, and fit my key into the crumbling lock. It turned, and I was outside, in the sun, in the wind, in the blowing flax and rye grass.

I shivered and could not stop. *You dumbo,* I told myself. *There was no one there.* "Snowy!" I yelled, walking into the stable. There was no answer. I saw something move from the very corner of my eye. A small brown rat tumbled into a hole beneath the straw.

I stood quite still for a moment. Nothing was wrong. *Just an old page on a calendar,* I said to myself. *Doesn't mean a thing.* I went into the stable. Into the first stall. I plunged my hand deep into the humus on the windowsill for my gun. It was gone.

Time lingered and spun by with no sounds in it, no movements. In my hand were two useless keys. Useless because if Rudy or Danny decided to jump me and fight me, I wouldn't have a chance in a million of getting away, fighting back, or being heard. I watched a spider make its way down a sun-frosted bit of web into a cistern in the corner. The cistern was full of ancient rainwater and fermented oats. It was about ten feet deep and would be a nice place to throw me after they'd finished beating me up. *Get out of here,* I told myself, but I could not will my legs to move. Where was my gun? Who had taken it? I leaned softly against the wooden wall of the stall.

All the sounds were innocent. A wisteria vine tapped against a windowpane. Pingings came from the cistern. Birds were warbling in the bushes outside. Deep in the walls I heard the scurryings of the rats and mice who lived there. I edged out of the stall, through the barn entrance, and into the sunshine. Then I just stood there idiotically and gazed up at the school.

"What the hell is the matter?" asked Snowy.

I turned as fast as a jackrabbit. "Snowy! Where *were* you?"

"You're as white as a sheet," said Snowy. "And your shirt is soaked through."

"Snowy, someone is on to us. Last fall I hid a pistol that my father gave me right in the dirt on the windowsill. It isn't there! In the old kitchen where I come through after class there's a calendar. Someone's changed the page."

"Barney," he said, "I've broken the code. The writing!"

"But my gun!" I was still shaking. "The page . . . "

Snowy spread my tracing of the little stone-carved figures out on the floor of the stable and knelt over it. "Exams have gotten to you, Barney," Snowy said seriously. "The tension's boiled your brains. Nobody's going to bother us."

"But Rudy? Danny? The other three? Where are they?"

"There's a big cookout tonight and a dance with a busload of girls from Lexington Country Day. Barney, do you remember the Lexington girls at the Columbus Day dance? Half a dozen of them could model bikinis. Remember Rudy hanging all over that blond, blue-eyed tall one with a body like . . . "

Snowy blushed. "Barney, these girls are playing softball in the quad in T-shirts. You think anybody in this sex-starved monastery is gonna miss out on that except us? Come on, man, you're getting paranoid. There's workmen and gardeners all over the campus. So one of 'em was down in the basement. So what? One of 'em probably found your gun and took it home. My listening monitor is on, Barney. If anyone was following us, I'd hear. Okay? Now look at this."

I settled my mind a little and stared at the puzzle in front of us. "How could you break the code?" I asked. "You have no other thing to go by. These aren't like Egyptian writings in the pyramids, where they made little pictures of birds and things. These are just marks. Shapes."

"That's what it looks like if you start from the beginning," said Snowy. "You started to trace at random, in the middle of the circle, Barney. Look. Your first marking is a loop with two darts. Means nothing like that. But if you start here, see, with the single dart, then it's two darts after that, then a triangle. Then a triangle and one dart, a triangle and two. Then a single inverted triangle."

"So?"

"It's a system of numbers. On the base of three."

Snowy pointed. "Every three digits the main sign changes. A triangle means three. An inverted triangle is six. A square is nine. A circle is twelve. A circle followed by a dart is thirteen, two darts fourteen, and then a new sign for fifteen, a cross."

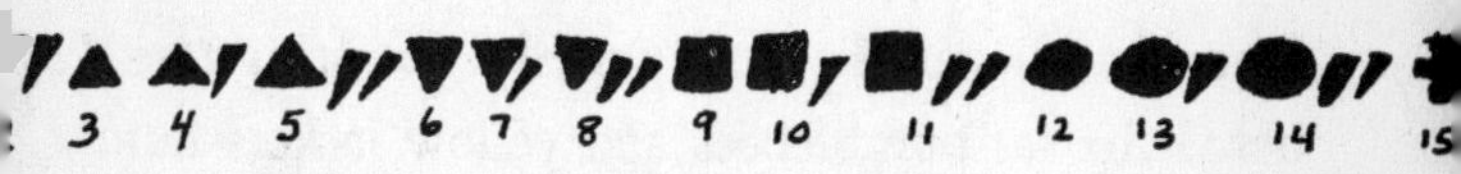

I read the little signs over and over as Snowy smiled, seeing the sense they made to me. Then he added, "I wouldn't have figured it out except it's an arena," he said.

"What? I don't follow."

"I thought at first it was word writing. Then I started wondering. Why should words be put on the sides of a stadium? Of course. They're numbered sections! Just like Fenway Park."

I shook my head slowly. "Snowy," I said, but I only thought what I wanted to say. That he was probably one of the world's true geniuses. Like some kid who gets hold of a violin when he's ten months old and starts playing Mozart.

"What?" asked Snowy.

"Let's get going."

Snowy blindfolded me, and we traipsed off. The woods were now full of summer leaves and colonies of frogs. I felt summer and heard it and smelled it, although I could see nothing but the black soccer shirt over my eyes. Skunk cabbages crushed under our feet. Gnats clouded around our heads, sparrows argued, and every time we passed a flowering tree, I heard the fat bumblebees and yellow jackets humming like toy battery motors around the branches.

"Do you still have your listening device on, Snowy?" I asked.

"Yup. Nothing comes through but the birds and the bees."

Suddenly I said, "Snowy?"

"What?"

"Are we going a new way? A different way?"

At first he didn't answer. Then he said, "I didn't think you'd know."

"Why are we going a new way?"

"Just in case," he said. "This is a noisier way. If anyone's following us, I should pick up their sounds."

"Hear anything?"

He snorted. "I don't think this thing was made for woods in the spring. There's too much other noise. Never mind."

Warm sunlight and soft cool shadows blinked

over us. I could feel them as I never did when I could see all around me. "Snowy," I asked him, "what are we going to do if we open up one of those little crypts and find a body made of bones the size of the one the collie found?"

"We're going to look at it," said Snowy.

"Yeah, but after."

"Nothing."

"Snowy, if it's true, if there was once a race of human beings a half a foot tall who had a whole civilization, a city, you could be the most famous person of the century for finding it! You could be rich! You'd be on the cover of *Time.* You might even get out of going to school forever!"

"Then it wouldn't be my cave anymore, Barney."

"But, Snowy, you can't keep something like this secret. It's too important!"

"Barney, no matter what we find today, you may take nothing out. Disturb nothing. And no blabbing about it."

Snowy had stopped walking. His warning was clear as the yammering of a blue jay that circled somewhere over our heads.

"You got it, Snowy," I agreed. I had no choice.

We slithered through the mud tunnel and into the first chamber. Snowy removed my blindfold, and we made our way delicately over the catwalk ledge that led to the slide, then we coasted down the chute and bumped to a stop on the frigid sand below.

Snowy lit the first lamp, I the second, and we walked in silence across the river and on to our last dig.

Everything Snowy had described to me was there and more. The paintings around the inner wall of the arena were done in browns and reds and blues. He had cleared down to the bottom of the temple itself.

"I think it's a religious thing," he said. "Look. All the columns have snakes except on the upper two tiers. Almost like a place reserved only for the gods at the top."

And there had been gods at the top. Their heads had all fallen off their pedestals, but they still lay in the bottom of the pit on top of a lake of inlaid silver cobra heads. They looked very much like our first statues, fierce and curly bearded, helmeted and terrifying.

"They must have had something like bullfights here," I said, squatting in the middle and feeling the delicate marble columns that held up the building. They were no bigger around than cigars. "Something like lion fights. Except with snakes." I stood. The temple was nearly twice as tall as I was. My eyes lit on the stone coffins that ringed the building. "Dead warriors?" I said.

"Looks like it."

"You mean it, Snowy? You'll open one up? How about four-thousand-year-old mustard gas?"

"I ordered two gas masks," said Snowy. "They didn't come yet. We'll take a chance. Don't breathe in."

I hesitated, kneeling before one of the raised stone graves. "Supposing there's nothing in it?" I asked.

"Then there's nothing in it," he said.

"Supposing there's a skeleton in it?"

"Then we leave it in peace."

He had brought a chisel and a jeweler's hammer. He slipped the chisel's blade against the seal of the tomb and tapped. I stopped him. "Wait," I said.

"What's the matter?"

"I heard something."

We had brought all five of our lamps around us. They gleamed like lights under water.

Snowy knelt, listening like a cat, head to the side, for a moment. "It's nothing, Barney," he said. "The cave drips, you know." He placed the chisel end against the tomb's seal and reached for his hammer. He tapped again.

But somewhere in the hush behind the dark I heard a giggle.

They had one big flashlight. They waltzed across the sand like five drunks. When Rudy reached the pair of man-serpent statues, he tried to lift one and, not succeeding, kicked it hard with his boot heel. I heard the black glass breaking. Matt and Danny found the potter's shed and tromped on it gleefully. "What have you been building, boys?" Shawn yelled. "A dollhouse village?"

They began running up and down the tiny street of shops and houses, crushing, kicking, and yodeling.

Once Rudy stopped and grinned at us. "You guys have fun making a little town here? I didn't know you still liked to play! I like to play too!" He stomped hard on the fountain in the Rich Man's House. "You two are really talented, boys! Talented and gifted! A miniature city, all made brick by brick by a couple of little cutie pies! What's in that big pit you're sitting in? You building a little church to go with the town so the itty-bitty pretend people can say their prayers? Or are you making it for Dr. Dorothy's guinea pigs to live in? Better watch out! The poor little guinea pigs might catch cold down here!" Rudy danced in the sand. The Rich Man's House was a shambles under his heavy boots.

Snowy fumbled in his pocket. He drew out my gun and, before I could move, crouched in a trooper's position, arms straight out, and fired it at Rudy Sader.

The gun clicked.

"Give it to me, Snowy," I said. "You don't know how to work it." I grabbed the gun from him.

"Get them, Barney. Get them!" He was crying for the village, for our secret, like a mother animal whose young is being tortured in front of her.

I slipped the little emerald on the gun's handle down and over. *Aim. Aim right, you fool, I told myself.* KAPOW! The glass of Rudy's flashlight shattered. Then I did the same with our five kerosene lamps. *Kapow!* The lamps exploded one by one. They went down the way penny arcade ducks fall, and the cave resounded with the shots in its sudden darkness. From the ceiling there was a great whirring. The piercing shrieks from squadrons of panicking bats filled the air all around like a thousand dog whistles.

Snowy took my hand in his and led me out. We slipped away, ourselves like snakes. A bat brushed my ear with its velvet wing. I heard the click of its steel-sharp nails as it flew by.

CHAPTER EIGHTEEN

I did not talk to Snowy on the way back. He'd blindfolded me as usual but sobbed so horribly, there was no good in my doing anything but being quiet. I did not cry. I was too angry. After a bit Snowy's crying died down, and I supposed he was thinking the same thoughts I was. About the bats ripping the hair off the boys. About them starving there for a week, about them running into the cobra teeth or just plain dying of fear and cold. I pictured Rudy on his hands and knees pleading. I pictured them calling for help and help not ever coming. I called him the filthiest name I knew.

I did not say anything until the turf underfoot turned to soft pine needles and I knew we were at the edge of the woods near the school.

"Snowy?" I said.

No answer.

"The hell with this!" I grumbled, and ripped off the black cloth over my eyes.

Snowy was gone. How long had I been walking alone?

I stumbled into the stable. What had happened and what was going to happen gurgled and milled and juggled around in my brain like a ten-colored pinwheel.

The boys would be missed whether I said anything or not. The police and fire rescue squad would spend the next month looking for the cave. Snowy would never give anyone a clue where it was. And where was Snowy? I knew he would disappear for a while. Then suddenly I knew very well where he was. He had seen me hide my gun, the first day I'd been in the stable. The old kitchen in the cellar was one of his hiding places. Snowy had changed the calendar. Snowy had stored his *Soldier of Fortune* mail order equipment down there. That explained all the loose Styrofoam. The Styrofoam couldn't have come from 1951. It hadn't even been invented back then. He had probably picked the locks to the old kitchen months before Finney gave me the keys.

I sat down on a dirty pile of straw and tried to think. I could not. My heart, stomach, and lungs welled up with anger like sickness. Again the image of a mother animal and her young returned clearly, this time of a mother raccoon, her cub shot dead at her feet by a hunter. I had witnessed that once. She had thrown herself on the hunter and bitten his leg to pieces. Up in the quad I heard faint music. I'd forgotten there was a dance and barbecue going on.

I wandered around the edge of the campus. My mind had emptied. The thoughts that wanted to start there couldn't get off the ground. I didn't have any idea what time it was until I realized that complete darkness had fallen, and because it was June, that meant it must have been somewhere around nine. I smelled food. I walked up to the quad, my hands in my pockets.

There was a rock band playing. Five musicians. I walked up to the grill and asked for a hamburger. The cook turned to face me. It was Silks.

The headmaster usually did the barbecue honors with a big chef's hat on for effect. Finney had loved it. Finney always gave you a hot dog with a flourish, as if he were handing you a plate of cherries jubilee.

Silks's eyes focused and saw me. He dropped his barbecue fork and whispered something to a woman tending a deep fry. Then he came around the table and placed both his hands on my shoulders. He began to push me.

He shoved me gently, without a word, into a dark corner of the main building, behind a pine tree. "Where are the boys, Barney?" he asked. I looked into his eyes. They were full of terror. Silks had never called me Barney in the three years I'd been at Winchester.

"What boys?" I said.

"Barney, Mr. Damascus is here tonight. He's come for graduation. Mr. and Mrs. Sader too. Their sons are missing. So are MacRea and Swoboda and Hines. Where are they? They haven't been seen for six hours!"

"How should I know?" I said, fascinated by Silks's voice and eyes. I had never heard him speak softly or seen him afraid.

"Barney, answer me. Your friend Clarence Cobb is not at the Finneys'. He's gone. Mr. Finney is very worried. Apparently Clarence had some kind of pet . . . a kitten?"

"A guinea pig," I stated flatly.

"Yes, well, Cobb and the guinea pig are gone. You know where those boys are, Barney. Please tell me."

"I'm hungry," I said.

Silks dropped his hands from my shoulders to his sides. "Go to my office. Please, Barney. I'll see someone brings you a hamburger and a soda. Go to my office."

I was unsure what to do. My intelligence was as feeble as a light bulb in a brownout. Where was Snowy? I stumbled over to the main building, went into the headmaster's office, and sat and waited for Martin Silks. Over and over one idea spun itself around and around: that the five boys who had wrecked everything we had spent months uncovering were still in our cave. Would they find the way out? I doubted it. Only Snowy knew where the recess in the cave wall was. The boys would sit in that cave forever. They would starve, freeze, or scare themselves to death. I wanted that to happen.

I heard footsteps clatter down the hall. I knew I was in a dream. An evil dream that would soon be over. While I waited in an uncomfortable plastic molded chair, I dug my fingernails into my face to see if I could wake myself up. I could think only of Snowy. Snowy and Rosie.

Silks brought me a hamburger. Medium rare.

While I was eating he sat outside at his secretary's desk typing something. When I had finished, he said only, "Barney, I will make it worth your while."

"What?" I asked.

"Barney, you know where they are, don't you?"

I didn't answer him. I couldn't handle the "Barney" from Mr. Silks. But I was beginning to come out of the dream.

Silks sat on the edge of his big Danish-modern desk, not behind it. He showed me a letter on Winchester Academy stationery. It was addressed to the dean of admissions at Hotchkiss.

The letter explained that due to a last minute change of plans on the part of my father I was not to attend school in Europe, and it asked that I be admitted to Hotchkiss in September. It said that I was a "significant student." It listed my grades for all three years as 4.0 including today's exams, which could hardly have been corrected yet. It said I was valedictorian of the class.

I just stared at the letter. I was positive I was back in the dream. "We don't have a valedictorian," I said.

"We do now, Pennimen," said Silks. "I thought I'd throw that in. These important schools like achievers. This letter is late, but it will get you in. Over the years more than a hundred boys have gone from Winchester to Hotchkiss." He dangled his leg, smiled, and placed the letter square on the desk, delicately, as if it were a gold bullion certificate. "If you want me to put in anything else—other interests? Anything?" Then, when I said nothing, he added, "If the boys have hurt you, Pennimen, I will discipline them. Just tell me where they are."

I didn't answer. I tried to create my father's voice in my head. I tried to listen to what he would tell me to do. Instead all I heard was the band outside the window and my own voice droning "If" for countless mornings in this office.

"Where are the boys, Pennimen?" he said sharply.

I said nothing.

"Would you prefer another school, Pennimen?" Silks asked anxiously.

"Mr. Silks?"

"Where are they? Pennimen?"

"Mr. Silks, are you making a deal with me?"

"Exactly. We've made deals before. Haven't we?"

"Yes, but I didn't do the deal."

"Well, this time you will, won't you?" He glanced jumpily out the window at the party. Girls and boys were dancing wildly. The music was too loud for me to think.

"I tell you where the boys are, and you get to keep your job, right?" I asked him.

"And you get to go to Hotchkiss," he said, "and with high honors, as valedictorian of your class, may I add?"

I squinted at him as if he were hard to see. "You

put in the letter that I had a four-point-oh average. Exams haven't been corrected yet."

Silks grinned. "Hotchkiss won't double-check," he said. "We're two of a kind, Pennimen." He extended his right hand. "It's the way the world works, boy."

I looked at his hand. I was listening to my own voice hanging in the air from other days. Oh, how I had hated "If." But the words of the first verse rang, singsong, in my ears and took on the beat of the rock drummer outside. Stupid, sappy, worn-out words. I despised them because Silks had made me say them over and over, but the poem haunted me in my own voice. *"Or, being lied about, don't deal in lies."*

"Barney," Silks repeated, his hand still outstretched to mine, "it's the way the world works."

"No, it isn't," I answered. The letter drifted from my hand to the floor.

Silks's voice became its usual sharp bark again. "All right, Pennimen. You stay put. I'm going to call the cops. I'm going to tell them you had something to do with the disappearance of five young men. Believe me, they'll get it out of you."

I did not stay put. While Silks went to the telephone I opened the window, the one Finney'd let me out when Rudy and his friends were at the door, and walked out into the middle of the party. A girl asked me to dance. I stared right through her. I wandered down to the stable again.

The sounds of the dance floated downhill from the school. "You rotten, dirty scum!" I yelled to the pattering rats and empty stalls. "You deserve to die, Sader. All you'll ever do in this world is destroy things." I called them names. I swore words I'd never said before. Then I got up and kicked in the partition between two of the old stalls, as if my feet and legs were axes and I were chopping down the building.

Finney found me, asleep on a pile of straw, at ten o'clock.

"Barney," he said, jogging my shoulder, "are you all right?"

I lifted my head and wiped the filth from my face. "What? What happened?"

"Barney. Snowy is gone. He has taken Rosie and her two babies with him. I don't worry about him. I know he's hiding someplace. But the five boys are missing. They were not at the cookout or the dance. They are not in downtown Greenfield. The police have been called. Where are they, Barney?"

My mouth was full of chaff. "Mr. Finney," I said, "I will not tell."

I saw the moonlight wink off Finney's glasses. He put his hands in his pockets and rocked on his heels. "I see," he said at last.

"Everything," I repeated. "They wrecked everything. Our little houses, the sheds. Everything. They were laughing, Mr. Finney. They thought it was more fun than a circus. They thought Snowy and I . . . " Here I nearly retched. "They thought we had *built* the place. Thought we were playing, like kids. Make believe."

"And what did you do?"

"I . . . my father gave me a gun, Mr. Finney. Early in the year when—"

"What? What gun? What did you do, Pennimen?"

"I shot out their flashlight. The kerosene lights. Then we left. Snowy must have gone off somewhere in the middle of the woods. I don't know. I was blindfolded. I couldn't see. I kept asking Snowy what we were going to do. See? And he didn't answer. I didn't even know he'd taken off until I got practically to the stable. The boys are still down there. When you go in the cave, you have to slide down a chute, sort of. It's too slippery and steep to climb up. Only Snowy knows the way out."

"You shot out their lights!"

"Yes."

"Did you want to shoot the boys instead?" he asked in a voice so low I could barely hear it.

I waited a minute to answer. "Yes," I said.

"But you did not."

"No. I should have."

"Where is the gun now?"

It was still in my pocket. I gave it to Finney. The silver peacock on the handle flashed a little in Finney's hands. A full moon was shining right in the hayloft window.

"Pennimen," said Finney, "it could take a month with ten state troopers to find that cave. Will you go back? Will you save those boys' lives?"

"I don't know the way," I said.

"If you did know the way, Pennimen, would you? Or would you leave them there to die?"

"Let them rot!" I said. "They'll go out in the world and mug old ladies in dark alleys, or they'll set a building on fire. They'll grow up and experiment on innocent animals. They'll beat their wives and kids. All those things you read in the papers. Mr. Finney, that's the kind of boys they are. You know that too. Leave them. Let them suffer for a change. Let them be on the other side of the fence."

"Why didn't you pull the trigger on them instead of the lights, Pennimen?"

"Because I was a chicken, that's why."

"No, Pennimen." Finney touched my shoulder firmly. "You didn't do it because you are made of different stuff from them."

Pulling his wooden leg under him, Finney lowered himself to the floor. He took my hand in his, ugly finger stump and all, and as he had in his office the day this all began, he locked his bird bright eyes on mine in the gossamer light of the early summer moon. "Go get them, Pennimen," he said.

"I don't know the way."

"Yes, you do."

Something I'd said that afternoon prickled at the back of my mind. I had asked Snowy why we were going a new way because . . . it wasn't the right way, it wasn't the way we'd gone before. How had I known? *The way out,* a voice inside me insisted. *You still don't know the way out of the cave. The dog,* my other self answered it quickly. *Take the dog like Snowy did. The dog led Snowy out the first time he went down. The dog knows the way.*

"What is it, Pennimen?" he asked.

I didn't answer.

"I'll have a policeman come with you."

"No."

"The boys are dangerous, Barney."

"I need Bonnie, Mr. Finney. All I need is Bonnie."

He left, with one more glance at me. I found myself at the border of the woods. Dr. Dorothy had brought the collie to me. My eyes were open to the dark. The moon did not filter between the leaves. Being able to see, and with a flashlight in my hand, I had no idea which way to go.

My blindfold was bunched up in my back pocket. I put it on, and I went the way we always went, the collie trailing happily at my heels. I didn't even feel out for trees. It took me no more time than it did following Snowy at the end of the string ahead of me.

I came to a stop at a certain point, pulled off the old soccer shirt, and opened my eyes. I turned on my flashlight. Embedded in the crotch of a tree, secured in the *Y* of the central branches, was a tiny strip of brightly colored striped silk, half the size of a stick of gum. I recognized it from *Soldier of Fortune.* A Distinguished Service medal. Snowy's marker. Had it belonged to his father? I guessed it had. Pulling the dog behind me, I went in.

I walked the ledge and came to the head of the slide. Then I yelled down it. "Are you there?"

It took a minute or two. I think it was Brett who answered. "Yes! Help! Are you the cops? The first-aid people?"

"Are you hurt?"

"One of us has a sprained ankle. Another guy got his head ripped up by a bat. He better get a tetanus shot. Help us! Who are you?"

"It's Barney Pennimen," I yelled, "and you better do just what I want you to do."

Silence answered this. Then, "Okay."

"I want to tell you something."

"Okay." Danny's voice this time.

"I have the Finneys' dog with me. Can you hear me?"

"Yes!" Echoing answer.

I am going to come and get you. Do exactly as I tell you. If you try anything, I'll sic the dog on your throats. Understand?"

"Yes!" Five voices at once.

You dirty cowards, I said to myself, and pulling an unwilling Bonnie behind me, I went down the slide. I flashed my light on and off quickly. "Walk ahead of me," I said. And then to Bonnie I yelled, "C'mon, dog, home! Out!"

She led me straight across the cave to a crevasse in the wall. There I found the tunnel Snowy had been so careful that I never find. I let the boys file out in front of me. They said nothing. They must have been as cold as men drowning in a winter sea, but I could smell them. I could smell their panic.

I led them through the tunnel, Bonnie straining at her leash. They said nothing. They filed out, only occasionally darting backward glances at the dog's snapping and snarling.

When I'd gotten them outside at last, I could hear them gulping for fresh air. I half expected them to scatter into the woods, but they didn't. "What's the matter?" I asked. "Go on home. Or go into Greenfield. I got you out. Now you're on your own."

Three of them whispered together. I couldn't see in the dark which three. But then it was Sader who spoke. "Don't know the way back, man," he said gruffly.

"But you followed us here."

"Yeah, well, we just went after you, like. Didn't pay too much attention to which way. Come on, man. You've gone this far. We don't know where the hell we are. I've gotta get a tetanus shot fast."

"And we gotta carry Danny," Brett added. "He can't walk on that ankle."

I decided to take them the most roundabout way I could think of, just to make sure they didn't ever come back. Bonnie tried to pull me the quick way, the regular way, but I held her leash tightly as she strained against it. I led them up in the hills and over a stream Snowy and I had never crossed. I back-tracked and circled for an hour, losing myself and them in a maze of trees, swamps, and brier thickets. They swore at me and yelled over and over that Danny could not make it.

"Sweat a little, boys," I sang over my shoulder.

Finally, standing in the middle of an open spot of ground, waiting for the boys to catch up, I decided to take them back. "Okay, Bonnie, home!" I whispered. She took off like a rocket. I was not holding the leash properly, and it flew out of my hand. I heard her plunge into the underbrush ahead of us. And so did they.

I wasn't quick enough. I had tried to fade into the darkness of the trees. Rudy caught my leg. I struggled free and ran in the opposite direction. I was cornered against a boulder. I saw him coming at me. I edged my way sideward along the boulder. The moonlight was too bright. There was no hiding. Shawn came at me from one side and Brett from the other. I sagged against the rock. "I saved you!" I shouted. "I saved your stupid, miserable lives. Leave me alone!" They kept coming. Rudy giggled. Then I felt it.

In the bottom of my back pocket was the jewelry box. I never had found the right moment to sneak the little fang back into its ring in the cave. I yanked out the box and held the empty cobra tooth up. I stood straight and shined my flashlight on it. The boys stopped for just a beat.

"Watch it, guys," I said. "Go on home now. This is a snake tooth. Inside the venom sac is poison. I lost a finger to one of these. Everybody knows it. If you come one step farther, I'll let you have it. You can break my neck, but if I get you with one scratch of this thing, your heart'll stop and it'll be all over. Be careful. Just be real, real careful of this tooth. Hear?"

I sat slowly, legs crossed, and watched them. They melted away into the woods like snow in spring.

I sat against the rock for a very long time, until the sounds of the woods returned to normal and I was sure the boys were gone.

Then, with only a flashlight in hand, I let the forest swallow me up for the last time. I knew that Snowy would go back to the cave very soon. I wanted to put the tooth back. I wanted to see what was left. And I wanted to open the crypt because I had to know what was inside.

I retraced my circles and stream crossings and

found the entrance to the cave again without much trouble. For the last time I crawled through the tunnel and padded carefully along the ledge and slid down the chute, as if it were a slide on a playground. Then I took off my shoes and sloshed across the river.

The boys had wrecked almost all of our carefully uncovered town. Their footprints were everywhere, but they had not found the gold disks or the temple of the snakes.

I replaced the tooth perfectly next to its mate in its ring. Then I made my way to our last dig.

The chisel and hammer were right where Snowy'd dropped them. I propped the flashlight on the first level of the temple, between two columns so that it shone just where I wanted, on the top of one of the tiny crypts.

I picked up the tools and, as gently as if I were prying open a sleeping baby's closed fist, I began to work.

Something stopped me. In the damp air I was certain I'd heard a faint sighing. A mist of silver ash crossed the beam of my light. There was no one else in the cave, no one at all. Of that I was certain. But was there someone in this small grave? The remains of a man from so long ago that the time in between his time and mine was like the mass of a huge mountain? Like Mount Everest. Like the enormity of an ocean. I put the chisel and the small hammer down.

Open it! Go on! Open it and see! the voice in my head nudged me. But I felt a heaviness inside me that had a stronger voice. I already knew the truth. It had been proved beyond any doubt in my mind that at some point in that black hole of time that came before my own birth, this cave had been lived in, built in, and died in. But it was Snowy's cave in the end, not mine. I didn't want to be the first to see inside the little crypt. I hadn't the heart to open it without him there.

"Good-bye," I whispered to the dust of whomever might lie buried there and to the cave itself.

Putting out my light, I stood, unafraid, listening to the swirling of the river and the beating of my pulse, alone on an island of ghosts.

My father and I spent the summer in India and Thailand, looking for certain kinds of headdresses, statues, and mother-of-pearl fans that were not easily available in good quality in the States. I wrote to Snowy, again and again, at Winchester, at the Finneys' with "Please forward" scrawled on the envelopes. I told him to write me care of American Express. As usual, Snowy did not answer.

My dad asked me, one night in a restaurant in Bangkok, if I was free to talk to him about the cave.

"I got the boys out" was all I told him.

"Ever find out where they're going next year?" he asked.

"Nope," I said. "So long as they're a hundred miles away from New Hampshire, I don't care."

"Barney," he said, "what was in the cave? Why did you go down there? What did you find?"

I shook my head. Toying with his fork, Dad let it go.

I figured Snowy'd disappeared, tough little soldier of fortune that he was. Then in late September, when the maples were red and orange and the New England afternoon as crisp as a new dollar bill, I opened my mailbox and found a letter with a Greenfield, Massachusetts, postmark. It said:

Dear Barney,

How is Exeter? I hear it's a hard school. How are the Finneys? Guess what! My roommate is Snowy Cobb again. He and I are friends. He lets me have my stuff out on the shelves, and I let him keep guinea pigs in the room. I am his assistant. Every afternoon he blindfolds me and takes me to a place I have promised never to tell about.

The reason for this letter is that I found this on the chest of drawers. Snowy says it belongs to you.

Yours sincerely,
Peter Mellor

Out of the envelope dropped Snowy's tree marker, the little Distinguished Service ribbon medal. I popped it into my shirt pocket and loped down to the football field.

It was Saturday afternoon. The grandstands on the football field were packed. I caught sight of Dr. Dorothy and Mr. Finney, who were sitting near the fifty-yard line. They waved, and I waved back. The drums rolled, and the band began to play "America the Beautiful." On the other side of the field sat rows of gray-uniformed cadets. Exeter was playing the Concord Military Institute.

I intended to yell my lungs out for Exeter. Rudy Sader was quarterbacking for Concord.

Rosemary Wells is the versatile, popular Edgar Award–winning author of more than fifty novels and picture books. Her suspenseful and absorbing young adult novels have consistently received starred reviews, and her acclaimed picture books include the *Max and Ruby* series. She grew up near Red Bank, New Jersey. She now lives in Westchester County, New York.